TOTALLY AWESOME MAZES AND PUZZLES

First published 2016 by Parragon Books, Ltd.

Copyright © 2018 Cottage Door Press, LLC
5005 Newport Drive
Rolling Meadows, Illinois 60008

All Rights Reserved

ISBN: 978-1-68052-413-0

Parragon Books is an imprint of Cottage Door Press, LLC.
Parragon Books® and the Parragon® logo are
registered trademarks of Cottage Door Press, LLC.

Written by William Potter and Becky Wilson
Illustrated by Steve Wood, Emily Twomey, Isabel Aniel, Lorna Anderson,
Samantha Meredith, Jean Claude, and Sophie Rohrbach

TOTALLY AWESOME MAZES AND PUZZLES

a b c

PaRragon.

Over 200 incredibly puzzling activities

Tech teacher

The school computer has caught a virus! It keeps repeating letters. Cross out all the letters that there are more than one of to see today's subject.

C	O	Z	J	B	S	Z	O	J	Z
A	F	O	B	J	F	J	H	O	B
F	B	M	F	O	J	B	C	Z	O
J	Z	C	Z	B	Z	O	B	S	C
O	C	F	B	F	O	F	Z	O	Z
Z	B	J	O	T	Z	C	B	F	C

Today's lesson is

....

Hidden treasure

Sophia the squirrel has one acorn, but she's forgotten where she buried the rest! Find another 12 hidden in the woods.

Sleepy puppy

Dozy the dog is dreaming of his favorite part of the rug. See if you can find it!

Big brother, Little brother!

I'm Little Liam. Copy me one square at a time into the larger grid to see what my big brother Giant Jake looks like!

Tool trouble

Peter the plumber has dropped his wrenches! How many of each color are in the pile?

Green ☐

Orange ☐

Blue ☐

Pink ☐

Purple ☐

swamp swap

This 'gator likes to lie in the water. Can you find 8 differences in her reflection?

Math Mystery

6 ☐ 6 = 12

15 ☐ 5 = 10

6 ☐ 3 = 9

12 ☐ 5 = 7

4 ☐ 3 = 7

Help me finish the sums by filling in the missing + and − signs.

Lost City

Follow the directions to discover the Lost Jungle City! Where is it on the map? Mark it by drawing an X.

1. From the Start, go up 4 squares.
2. Move 5 squares toward the Thorn Forest.
3. Go up 3 squares, then 2 squares right, then up 2 squares.
4. Go 2 squares toward the Pitless Bottom.
5. Move down 1 square, then left 4 squares.
6. Go down 6 squares.
7. The Lost Jungle City is 4 squares right of here!

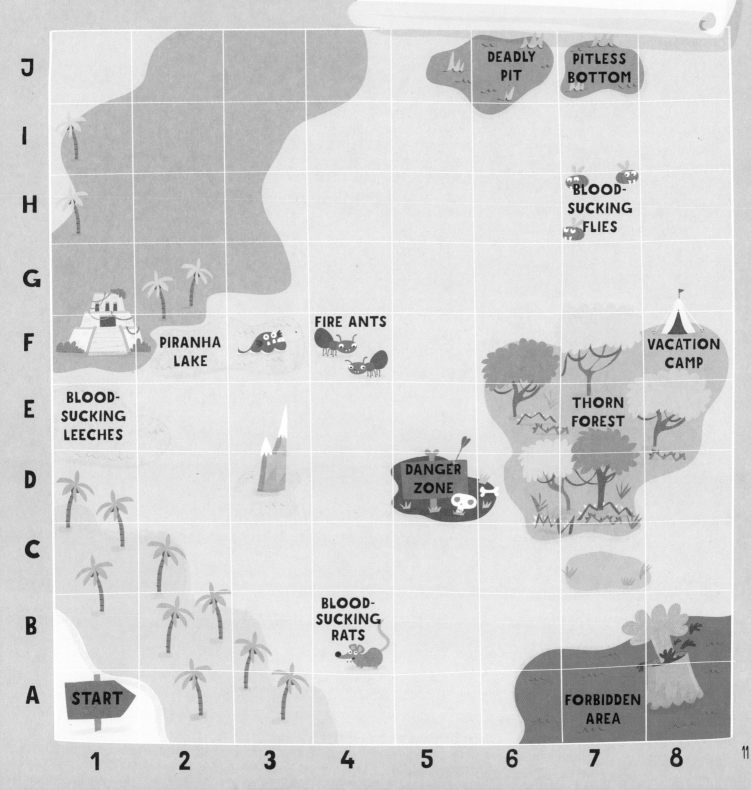

Ella is doing a survey of the coral reef...

Help her find:

10 shells

9 crabs

8 seahorses

7 shrimp

6 clownfish

5 butterfly fish

4 moray eels

3 trumpet fish

2 octopuses

1 lost diver's mask

Alien attack

Uh-oh! The aliens are planning an attack!
Color in the dotted shapes to find out
which planet they plan to strike.

vacation halves

I've been on so many vacations I can't remember where I've visited!
Fill in the stickers with the names of all the places I've been by joining two word halves from below.

Perfect pairs

Each of these words has an opposite. Draw lines to join the pairs of opposite words.

SLOW

YOUNG

COLD

LIGHT

DRY

DIRTY

WET

TALL

FAST

HOT

HEAVY

SHORT

OLD

CLEAN

Missing toppings!

Each pizza topping has a number value from 1 to 5. Draw toppings onto slices 2, 3, and 4 to make the toppings on each slice add up to exactly the same number as slice 1.

1
2
3
4
5

2
1
3
4

Monster change

Dr. Jangle drank a potion that turned him into Mr. Hideous! Order the pictures from 1 to 9 to see the change.

Copy street

Mr. Mirror wants his house to look exactly like his neighbor's.

He has everything he needs to build it, but which THREE parts does he NOT need?

19

This monster ate the menu!

Cross out all letters that appear twice, then unscramble the rest to see what he's ordered.

J M U S C A E J C K M U S

Now quickly draw it here—before he eats the table!

How many cakes and cookies did you draw on the stand?

Someone's been snacking at the birthday feast before the guests have arrived.

Happy

Birthday

Silly Circus

It's audition time at the
Superstar Circus! Can you find:

9 balls

9 yellow stars

8 saucers

6 hoops

10 cups

5 red noses

4 juggling pins

2 buckets

2 giant shoes

1 rabbit

shadow star

This singer is in the spotlight,
but which shadow matches her exactly?

A

B

C

D

E

Penguin puzzle

Hop this little penguin home across the different-shaped icebergs in this order:

You can go vertically or horizontally but not diagonally.

1 2 3 4

Start!

Home →

Finish!

Bird spotting

Match these rare birds with their pictures in the bird-spotter's guide, then color each with the correct pattern.

Bumble Jumble

Can you find Buzz? He's the only bee not part of a pair!

Odd robot out

Oops! There's a problem at the robot factory. Can you spot the robot that doesn't match?

Lost in space

Astronaut Aiden has forgotten where he parked his spaceship. Starting from Aiden, follow the arrows by the number of squares marked on each arrow to find the ship.

Start

Aiden

Example

find und squeuk

START

FINISH

Ginger the cat has lost her favorite toy!
Guide her through the maze to find it.

Dotty dress

Connect the dots to find out what's on the runway at this year's fashion show.

Then color in my new outfit!

Brave Cave Explorers

This creepy cave is full of letters!

```
        B W T B R S T
      T S M I O O Z E L Y H D S
    S M E L L T W A E D I S P I D E R
      W K U F E H D R A M X G A R V
        W G C V I N C R E E P Y Q
          W S C A R E K D B P G
            H O W L D H R G R
              W E Q F N I E
                B S T R P
                B A T
                S
```

Find these words:

BAT	SCARE
BITE	SLIME
CREEPY	SLUG
DARK	SMELL
DRIP	SPIDER
HOWL	TOAD
OOZE	WEB

costume calamity

Zap Man protects Super City from evil—but his costume is dirty! Which of these clean costumes is a replacement?

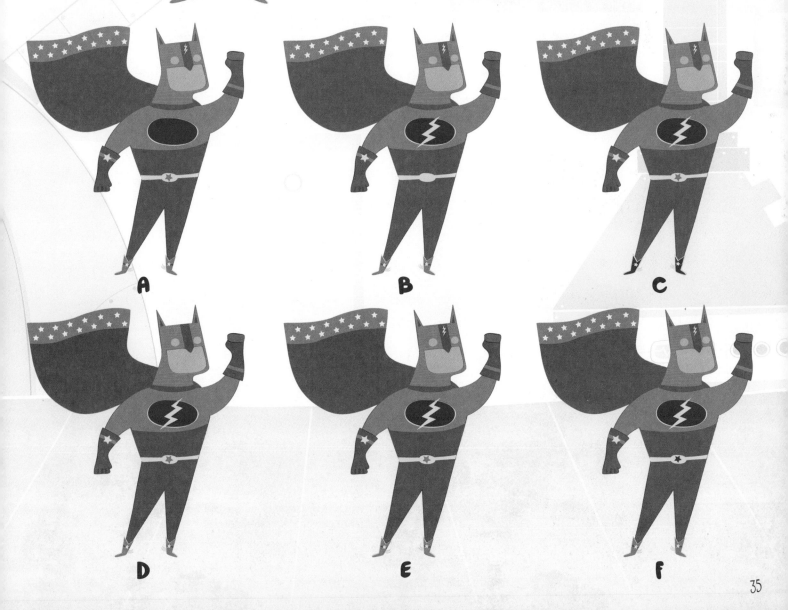

A

B

C

D

E

F

Science Explosion

The laboratory is disappearing! Quick, write the number of the correct missing piece in each gap to fix it!

Who has been Scrambled?

Copy each square into the correct section of the grid below to find out.

Pattern picker

What comes next in each pattern? Check the box under each correct picture.

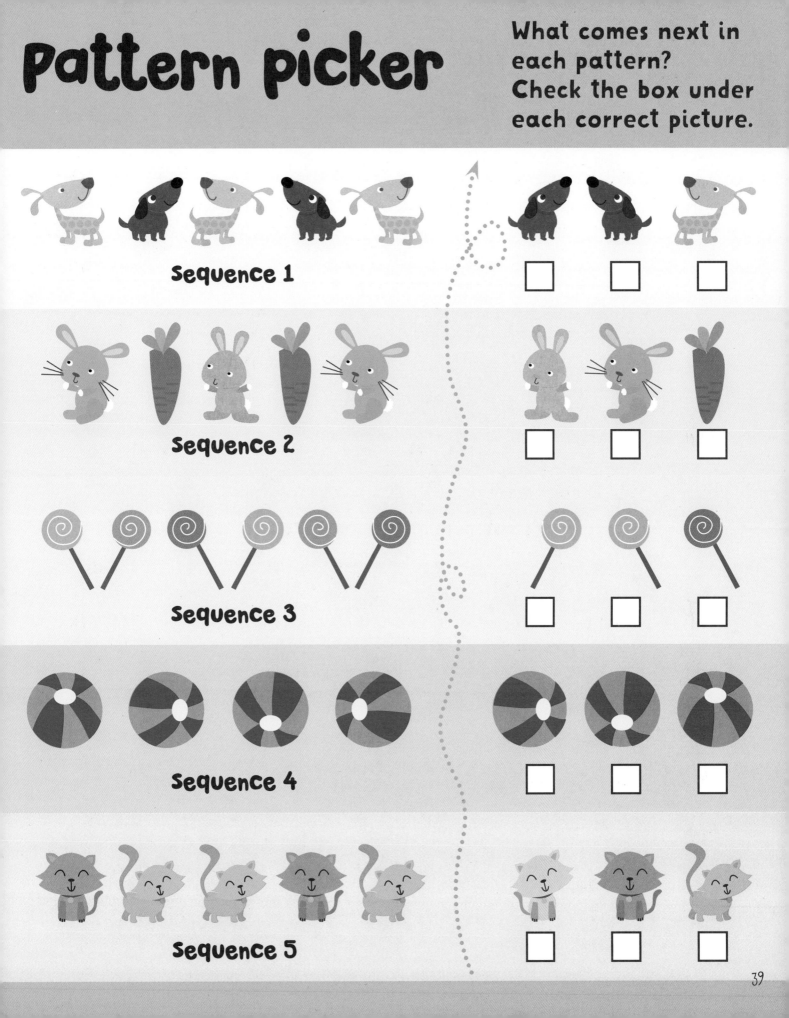

Sequence 1

Sequence 2

Sequence 3

Sequence 4

Sequence 5

four friends

We do everything as a group! Can you find us standing together in the crowded grid?

40

Number web

Spinderella the spider loves to eat flies! Fit the numbers into the spaces in the grid so she can keep track of how many she's eaten.

43
48
258
354
426
2004
5886
6623
86564
6023568
9083157

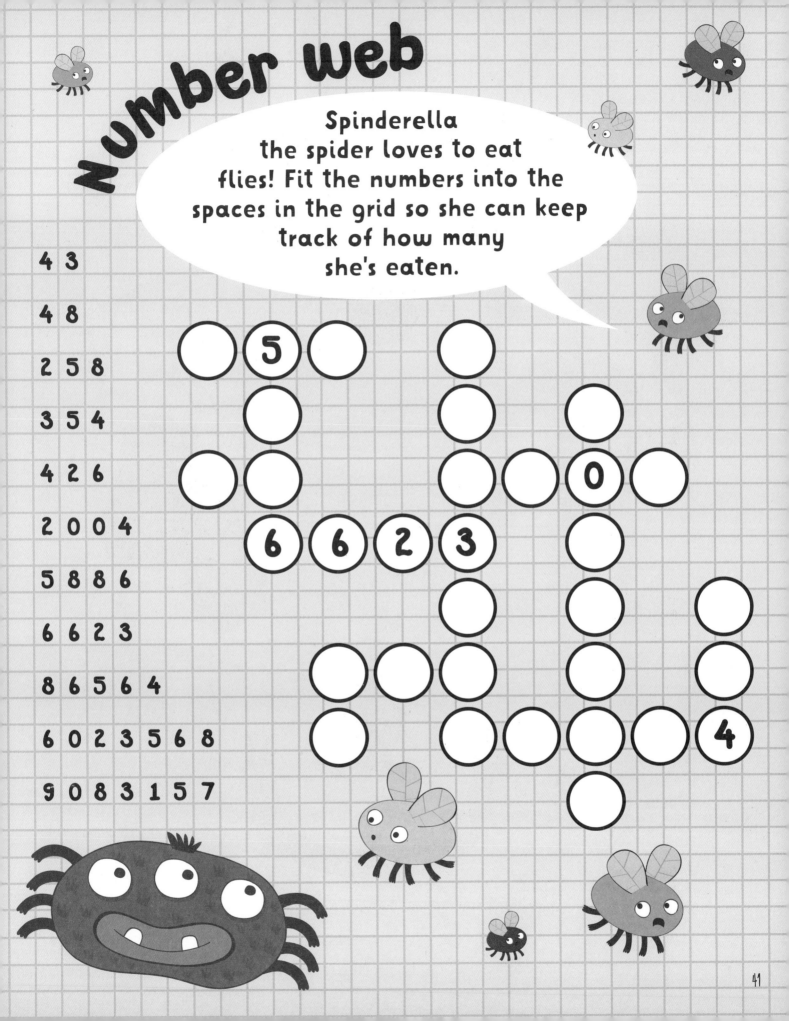

Dance away

Bobby pins

Apple

Dance shoes

Tights

Hairband

Dance shoes

Leg Warmers

Purse

Comb

Water

Emily needs to pack a bag for her dance class. Look at the things she needs for one minute, then turn the page and see if you can remember them all!

Dotty Dessert
Connect the dots to reveal a delicious dessert!

43

Odd one out

Clara loves collecting, but there is one thing that doesn't belong in each of her collections. Draw a circle around each odd one out.

1

2

3

4

What am I?

Which six different animals have been put together to create me? Label each of my parts with the name of the animal it came from.

Head ......

Wings

Nose

Tail

Body

Tongue

secret formula

This experiment is nearly done! Which test tube will my secret formula end up in?

W   x   y   z

seaside slices

It's a lovely day to be by the sea, but this sunny snapshot has been cut into slices! Figure out the order it should be in, from left to right.

The correct order from left to right is:

H _ _ _ _ _ _ _ _

It's a jungle jumble!

Some of these amazing animals have never been seen before.

Which five creatures are not shown in the guide below?

Jewel journey

I've been given a new tiara for my birthday! Lead me to it by hopping across the gems in this order: ♦♦♦♦ Move forward, backward, up, or down.

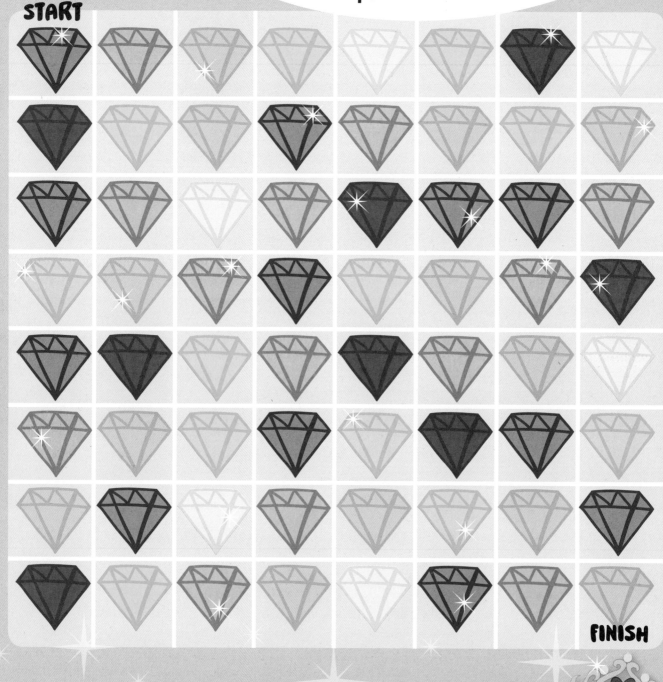

Go fish

How many fish can you find in this bowl?

Magic words

Find all these magical words in Wanda's cauldron.

BOIL   MAGIC
BROOM   SNAIL
CAT   SPELL
FROG   TRICK
GREEN   POTION
HAT   SPIDER

```
      R L E B
    P O T I O N O S
  L U T G R E E N E P B P
  N A O T S B T I F E R G
T B O I L F P R Y O L O N F
U I M C R U S I A R L O R E
  S P O A L N C D M I M S
  T G L O T A K H E A P H
    M A G I C A F R
      H L E T
```

Best bubbles

Which mermaid has blown the most bubbles?

....

Shelley

Coral

Marina

Dinner time

Yum! I've gobbled up three kinds of fruit. Unscramble the letters within each color to spell out their names.

E P E
P G
A P L R R
A A N
E O
P

The snake ate:

This mini-monster has a strange name:
MELLIFANGO
How many words can you make from it?

Write them all here.

1 ....
2 ....
3 ....
4 ....
5 ....
6 ....
7 ....
8 ....
9 ....
10 ....

11 ....
12 ....
13 ....
14 ....
15 ....
16 ....
17 ....
18 ....
19 ....
20 ....

How did you do?

0-5 words:
Shrunken brain!
6-10 words:
Monstrous mind!

11-15 words:
Scary smarty-pants!
16+ words:
Ghastly genius!

Bug hotel

Yikes! This room is full of creepy crawlies! How many times can you find the word BUG? Write your answer in the picture frame.

Don't forget, it could be written forward, backward, up, down, and diagonally!

B	G	U	B	B	G
G	U	B	U	G	U
U	B	G	G	U	B
B	U	G	U	B	U
U	G	U	B	B	G
G	U	B	U	G	B

Chimp Challenge

These clever chimps have figured out how to reach the highest bananas. Figure out what number is on each chimp by adding up the numbers on the two chimps immediately below.

Double Dance

These dancers are getting ready for the opening night!
Spot 10 differences in the bottom picture.

Super spotting

It's playtime in the jungle, but which leopard has the most spots? Check off your answer!

A

B

D

C

E

F

A ☐
B ☐
C ☐
D ☐
E ☐
F ☐

Hide and seek

When no one is looking, the fairies come out to play! Can you figure out where each of these photos was taken and then find the fairies hiding in the garden?

What do fairies like to eat?

Fairy cakes!

pirate puzzle

One-Eyed William the pirate has lost his ship! One silhouette matches his drawing of it. Which one?

Ahoy there!

A new dinosaur fossil has been found. Connect the dots to reveal the skeleton, then name your dino!

find a fossil

This is my
....................saurus!

Slippy scarf

Everyone is making the most of the snow.
But which rabbit has left a scarf behind?
Follow the trails backward to find out.

speedy snails

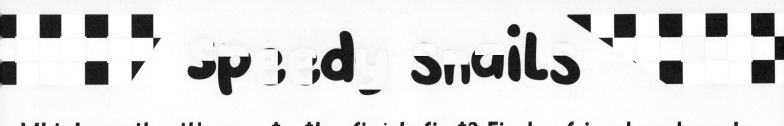

Which snail will race to the finish first? Find a friend and each get a pencil. Choose a snail each, then put your pencils on the start line. Race your pencils down the tracks to see who can lead their snail to the finish line first! Ready, set, **GO!**

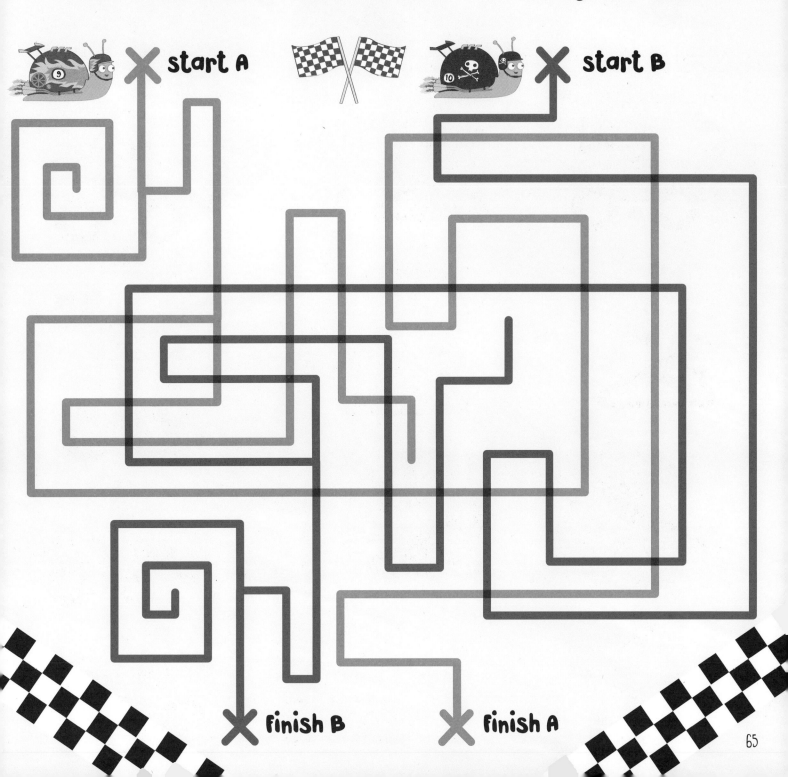

start A

start B

finish B

finish A

Digger repair

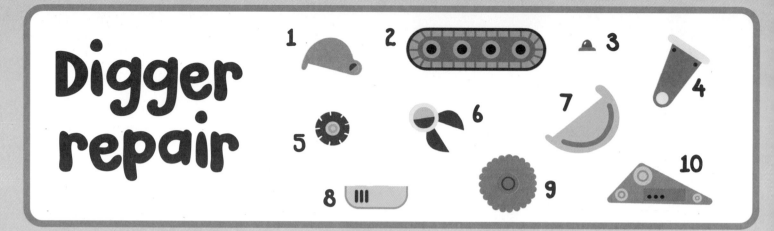

1 2 3 4 5 6 7 8 9 10

It's repair time on the building site! Each of the 10 spare parts belongs to one digger. Which two diggers don't have spares?

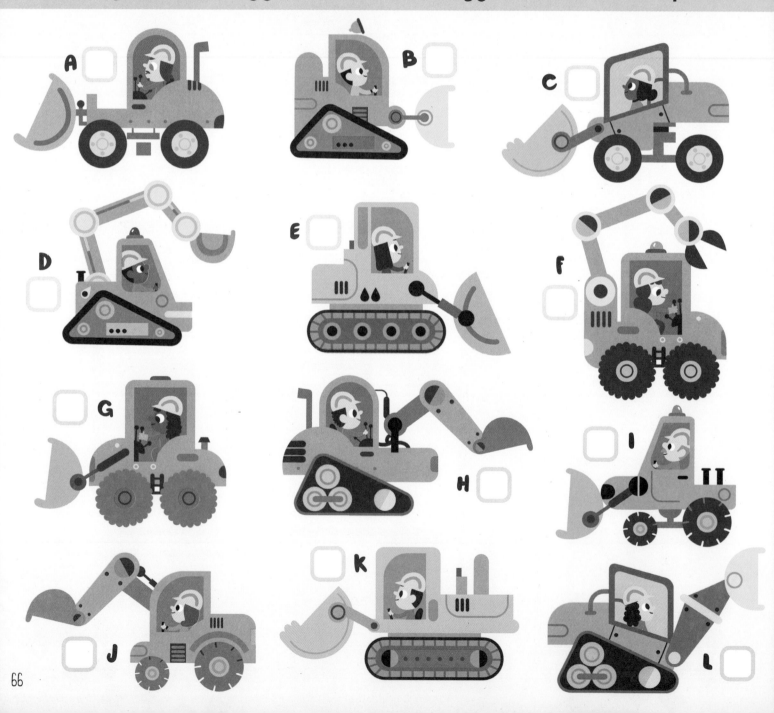

Big feast

- ☐ Bananas
- ☐ Apples
- ☐ Strawberries
- ☐ Pineapples
- ☐ Carrots
- ☐ Oranges

Gavin the gray bear loves all kinds of food. But what does he have the most of? Count the fruit in his dinner to find out.

A   B   C   D   E   F

It's the big race! Look at the pictures in the circles. Which number boat is shown in each circle?

Badger boat race

68

Princess patterns

Princesses love to play number games!
Figure out the missing numbers in each row.

A: 14 | | 10 | | 6 | 4

B: 5 | | 15 | 20 | | 30

C: 1 | 2 | | 8 | | 32

D: 1 | 2 | 4 | 7 | | 16

Aztec Mystery

Professor Bingley is unlocking the secrets of Montenumba's Temple! Figure out the numbers on each stone by adding up the numbers on the two stones immediately below.

10   11

2   8   3   6   9

It might take years to crack this code!

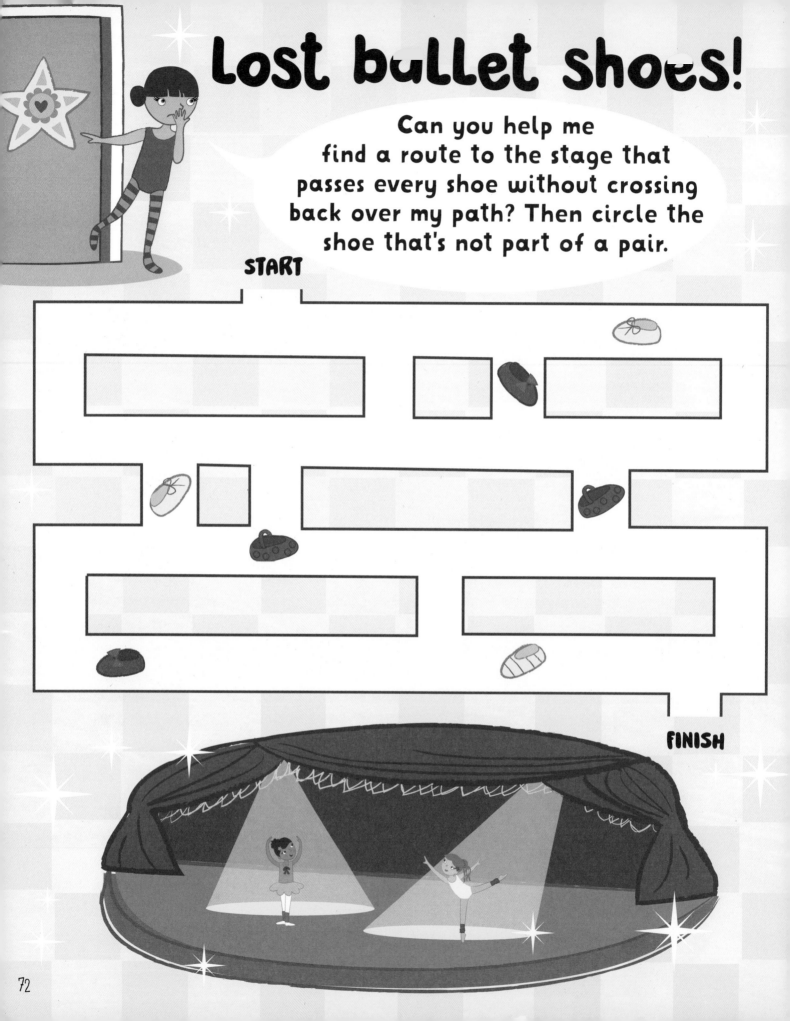

Lost bullet shoes!

Can you help me find a route to the stage that passes every shoe without crossing back over my path? Then circle the shoe that's not part of a pair.

START

FINISH

72

Sporty slip-ups

Something's wrong at the World Sports Championship.

Can you spot 12 things that aren't right in the stadium?

75

Duck Crossing

These ducks don't like to get their feet wet!
Find a way across the river, using the even-numbered stones
only and without going backwards.

shoppers!

Find and check off all the items on the list.

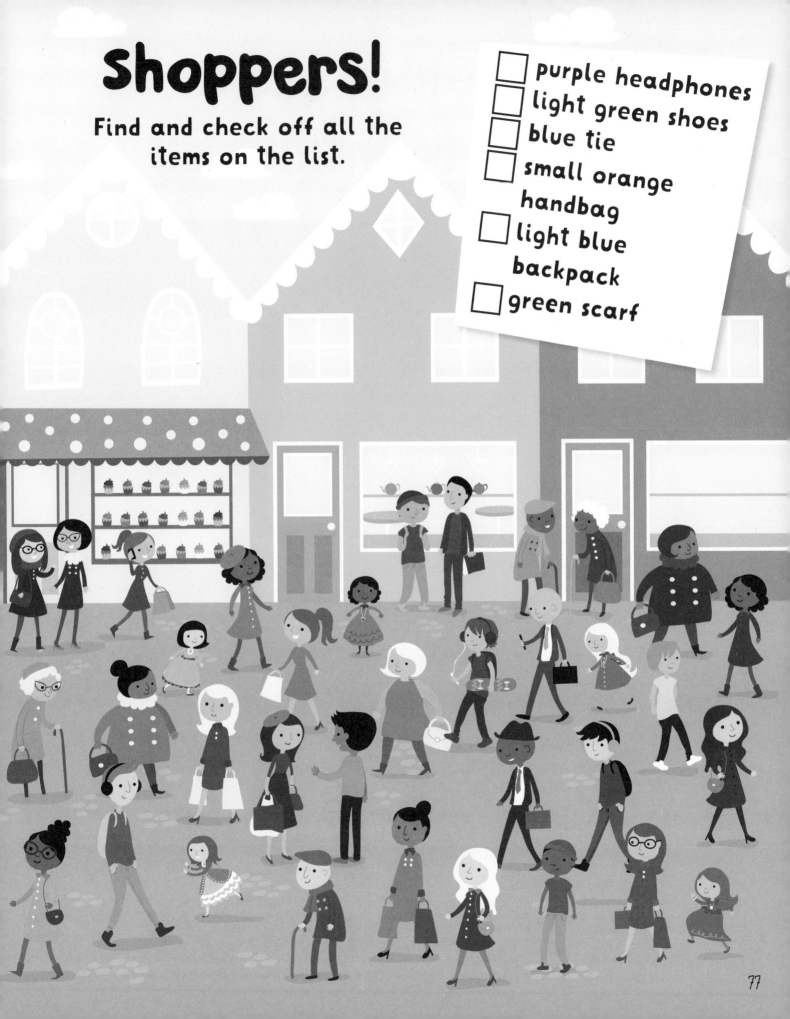

- ☐ purple headphones
- ☐ light green shoes
- ☐ blue tie
- ☐ small orange handbag
- ☐ light blue backpack
- ☐ green scarf

Monster Munchies

Find a path through the food following the above order
You can move one square at a time, up, down, and across, but not diagonally.

start

finish

Buried treasure

The most valuable
coin only appears once.
Which one is it?

Bella ballerina

What will Bella wear today?
Find the dress that matches her description.

I want a dress with a bow. It should have spots. No stripes. I want some red on it. Can the dress have a belt, too?

castle copy

King Norbert's castle has been smashed in a big battle. Rebuild it by copying one square at a time, using the numbers to help you.

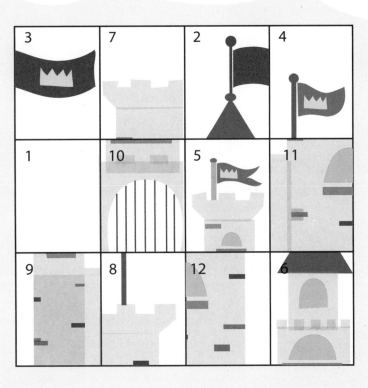

1	2	3	4
5	6	7	8
9	10	11	12

Dot-to-dot do!

Join the dots to reveal some wild haircuts.

Plane trails

Follow the trails behind each plane to spell the name of the countries they're flying to.

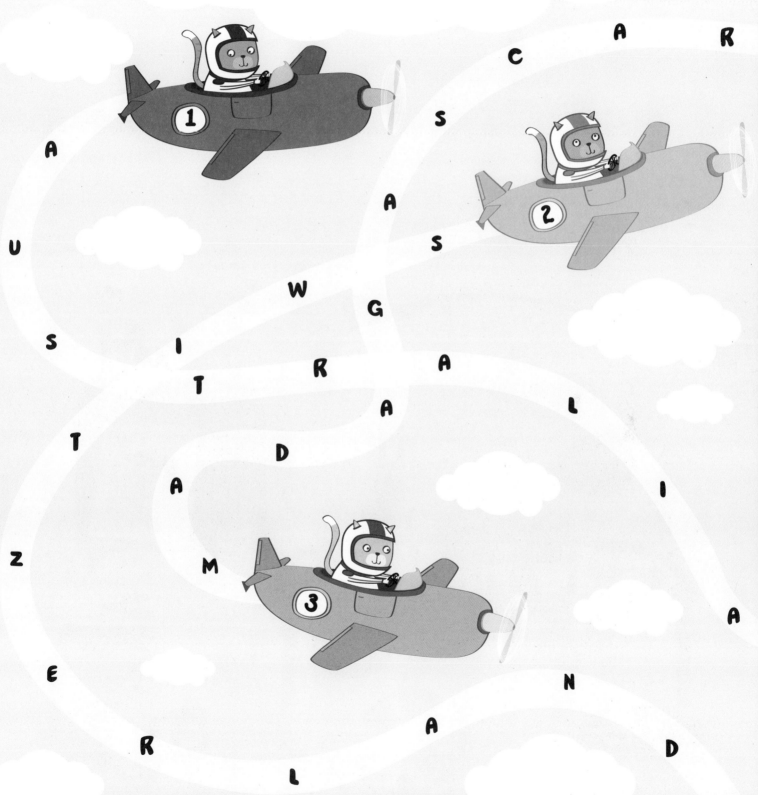

Justin's bedroom

Justin's bedroom is **SO** messy, he can't find his favorite toys and clothes! Can you?

Check off the items as you find them.

- [ ] **9** pens
- [ ] **7** toy cars
- [ ] **6** action figures
- [ ] **5** dinosaurs and prehistoric reptiles
- [ ] **4** pairs of shoes
- [ ] **2** toy helicopters
- [ ] **1** football

85

Robot xt-003

Circle five parts that are missing
on this robot's right side.

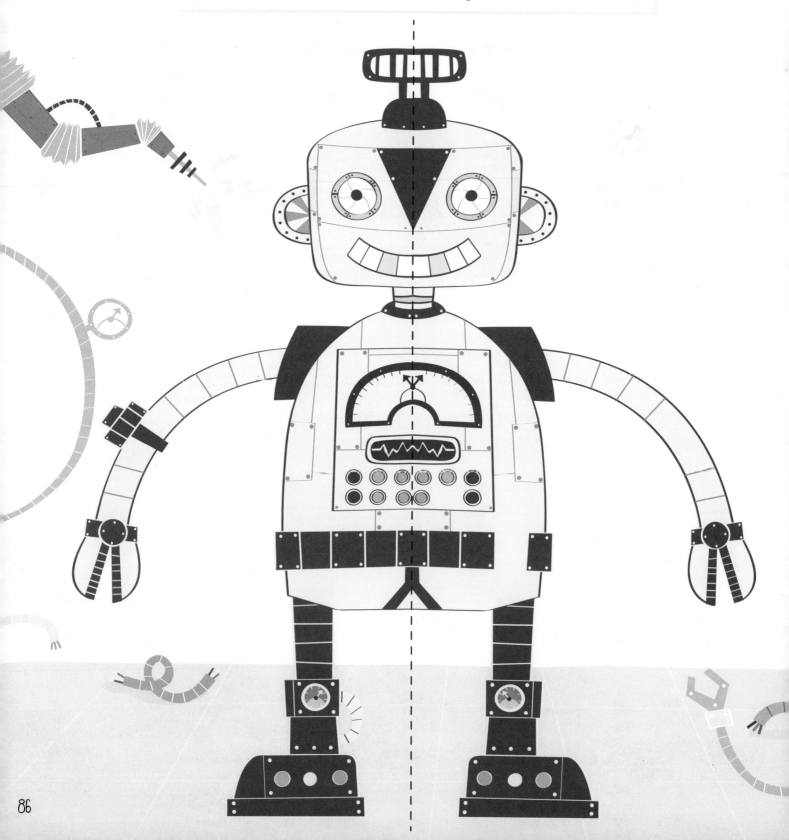

which way?

Which route should I take to park the tractor in the barn?

A

B

C

Baker Gallery

Francis Baker is painting fakes of famous paintings, but he's not very good. Spot one mistake in each of his fakes.

original

Whale maze

Ben Barracuda has been accidentally swallowed by the whale. Show him a way out of the whale's mouth so he can swim free.

finish

start

forgetful freddy!

Where is Freddy's car?
It's slightly different from all the other models.

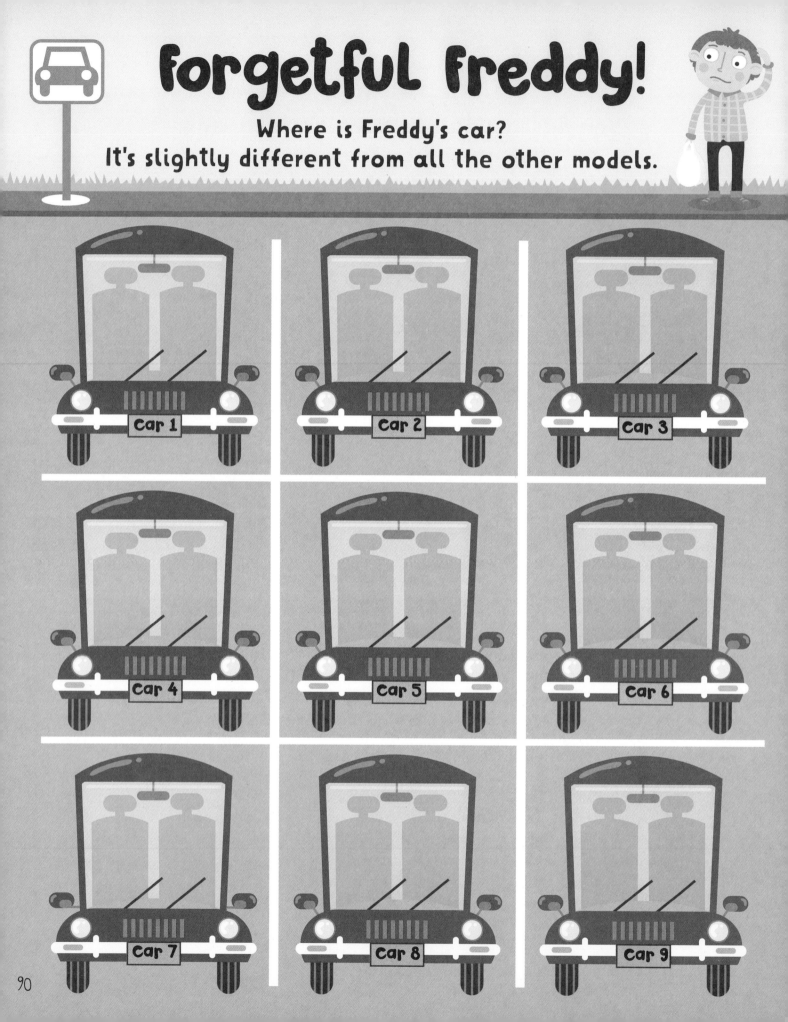

Car 1

Car 2

Car 3

Car 4

Car 5

Car 6

Car 7

Car 8

Car 9

Crowded bus

30 MAX   SCHOOL BUS   30 MAX

Mason wants to get on the school bus, but there are
only 30 seats. Count the children already aboard
to see if there is room for him.

Which weather?

fog   Sun   Ice   Wind   Snow   Rain

Draw lines to match each item with
the right weather.

93

Purr-fect match

Match each white cat to the black cat which has the same pattern.

Departures

DESTINATION

ANSWERS

S I P A R

H N A G S N W I T O

M O R E

C O M O W S

N L N O D O

B U L I N D

Unscramble each word to find out where each plane is flying. Use these stamps as clues if you need to!

PARIS FRANCE

MOSCOW

ROME

WASHINGTON

LONDON

IRELAND

Dance-off

Can you figure out which dance move comes next?

Draw your answers below

Owl match

Tonight the trees are full of owls. Find all the matching pairs.

98

castle confusion

My castle is missing five pieces! Compare both sides, then find five parts that are missing from the right-hand side.

99

Bug hunt

100

Space Search

Can you help the starship find all these words on the asteroids? Look up, down, and across.

```
B R K C Q O O Z O V C A I O L N A C X V
V V E N U S M M S A T U R N S U B O C G
B A S Z T A A A E P O F G Y Z L V M S W
V C R S P A C E D J G X F U H H S E R B
Y P Z W E P F J L C H D M Y B T N T M U
O Q L M D V J P G X D E M Y V R E I O E
A U H S C F F L O V R U D P J A D Q O Q
V R T R R J D A G M U P Z W F E W U N L
E A Q A B I J N S V B L R E T J Y D Q H
H N U M R D W E Q N E P T U N E J S Z A
R U P R K P V T E P Q R Z B Y Q U U W J
H S J U P I T E R L V X S T A R A I H O
```

Toy box

We always stick together! Can you find us sitting in this exact order in the toy box?

Dragon day

Mama Dragon's baby is hatching!
List the pictures in the
right order to show the baby
breaking free of his egg.

Egg _ _ _ _ _ _ _ _ _ _ Dragon

103

sail away

It's a beautiful day aboard the cruise ship! But can you find 9 differences in its reflection?

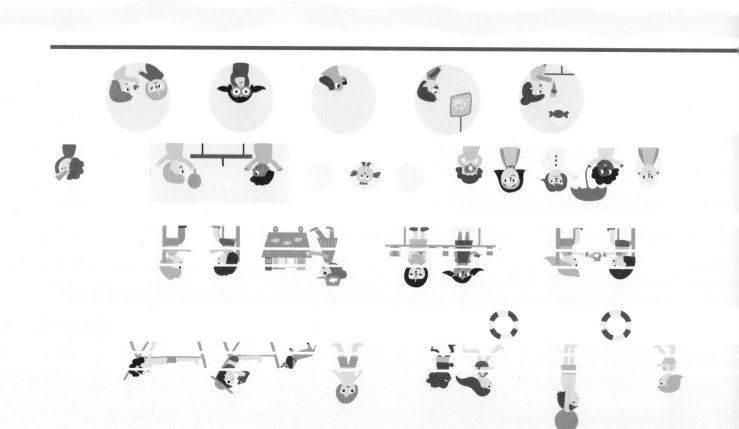

Ready to rock!

Which rock-star pieces fit into the concert scene? Write the letters in the spaces.

A

B

C

D

E

F

G

H

I

J

Butterfly beauties

106

There are

_____

Pairs of butterflies.

107

sky high

Animal halves

Use the word parts from the bottom of the page to finish the zoo signs!

GOR_____

_____HANT

___KEY

SK____

__ON

___TURE

BO___

SCOR_____

LI

PION

VUL

MON

ELEP

UNK

ILLA

AR

Time out

Can you re-build Princess Ticktock's grandfather clock from the broken parts?

Top __ __ __ __ __ __ bottom

midnight magic

Where do all the missing pieces fit in this sleepy scene?

1 ☐
2 ☐
3 ☐
4 ☐
5 ☐
6 ☐
7 ☐
8 ☐

Missing music

Which cello is mine? Match the silhouette to find out!

The instrument that matches is

creepy creature

Oops! I've magically mixed up these six creatures. Help me figure out what they were so I can change them back.

The creatures are:

1 ....

2 ....

3 ....

4 ....

5 ....

6 ....

flushed away

START

Oops! Princess Jinx has dropped her favorite ring! Find a path through the plumbing to return it to her.

FINISH

which bike?

Read the descriptions to figure out whose bike is whose!

fairground fun

Fill in the blank spaces on the big wheel so that each pair of numbers joined through the middle adds up to 16.

flower power

It's springtime in the park.
Find these three special flowers
in the colorful display:

Snip Snap

Who's new at the zoo? Connect the dots to find out, and colour them in!

Answers

p4 - MATH

p5

p6

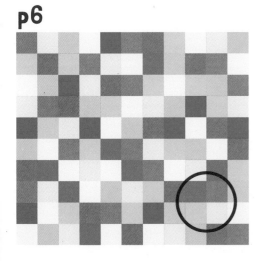

p8 - 3 green, 2 orange, 3 blue, 2 pink, 2 purple

p9

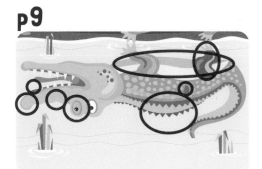

p10
$6 + 6 = 12$, $15 - 5 = 10$, $6 + 3 = 9$
$12 - 5 = 7$, $4 + 3 = 7$

p11 - C6

p12 - 13

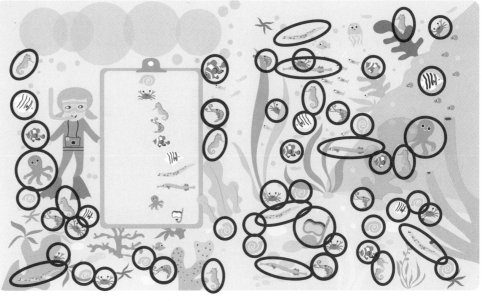

p14 - PLANET EARTH!

p15
AUSTRALIA   GERMANY
BRAZIL   MEXICO
CANADA   JAMAICA
ENGLAND   FRANCE

p16
SLOW and FAST
SHORT and TALL
LIGHT and HEAVY
WET and DRY
HOT and COLD
YOUNG and OLD
DIRTY and CLEAN

p17 - Slice 1 = 8. More than one way to make the other slices add up to 8.

p18

p19

p20-21 - The monster ordered CAKE.
You need to draw:
3 muffins, 3 cupcakes, 4 cookies

p22-23

p24-25

p26 - Shadow D

p27

p28

p29

p30 - Robot F

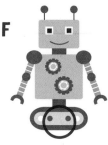

p31 - Spaceship C

p32

p33 - Your dot-to-dot should reveal a fashionable mini dress!

p34

p35 - Suit E

p36 - 37

p38

p39

1. dog
2. carrot
3. lollipop
4. ball
5. cat

p40

p41

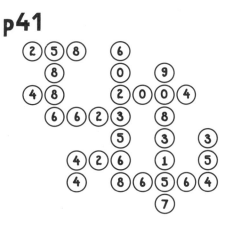

p43 - Your dot-to-dot should reveal an ice cream sundae!

p44

p45 - Head – lion; tail –scorpion; body – gorilla; tongue – snake; nose – elephant; wings – bat

p46 - Test tube X

p47 - H, C, F, B, G, D, A, I, E

p48 - 49

p50

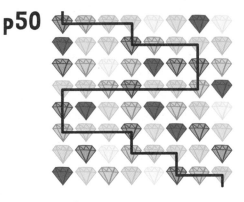

p51 - 16 fish

123

p52

p58

p67

6 bananas
5 apples
7 strawberries
5 pineapples
6 carrots
6 oranges

Strawberries are his favorite.

p53 - Coral blew 34 bubbles. Marina blew 19 bubbles. Shelley blew 15 bubbles. Coral blew the most bubbles.

p54 - ORANGE, APPLE, PEAR.

p55 - You could have: AM, GO, IF, MA, NO, ON, AGE, FIN, FOG, ILL, LEG, LOG, MAN, MEN, OIL, FALL, FAME, FELL, FLAG, FLEA, FLOG, FOAM, FOIL, GAME, GOLF, GONE, LEAF, LIFE, LIME, LOAF, LONG, MALL, MEAL, MILE, MOLE, NAME, ANGEL, FLAME, FLING, GNOME, FLAMINGO.

p56 - The word **BUG** appears 22 times.

p57

```
        48
      20  28
     8  12  16
    3  5  7  9
   1  2  3  4  5
```

p59 - Leopard F with 12 spots.

p60-61

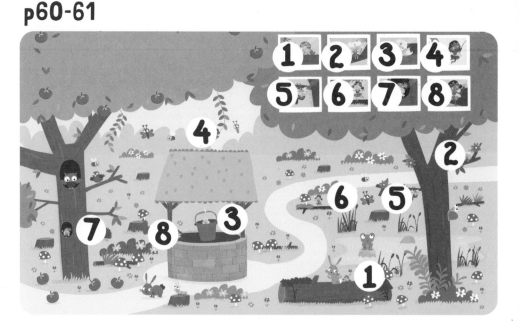

p62 - Ship D

p63 - Your dot-to-dot should reveal a giant dino skeleton.

p64 - Rabbit E

p66 - C and H don't have spares.

p68

A 14
B 21
C 11
D 15
E 05
F 12

p69

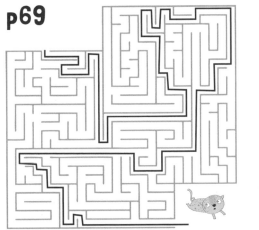

p70

A 14, 12, 10, 8, 6, 4
B 5, 10, 15, 20, 25, 30
C 1, 2, 4, 8, 16, 32
D 1, 2, 4, 7, 11, 16

p71

```
          85
      41     44
   21    20    24
 10    11    9    15
2    8    3    6    9
```

p72

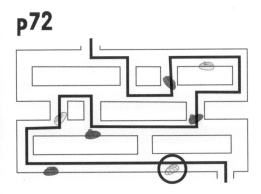

p73

p74-75

p76

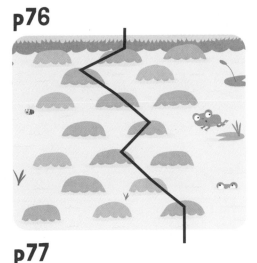

p77

p78

(dot-to-dot maze image)

p79

p80

(swimsuit image)

p82 - Your dot-to-dot should reveal one spiky hairstyle and one very tall hairpiece with a bow!

p83
1 Australia
2 Switzerland
3 Madagascar

p88

p84 - 85

p86

p87 - Track C

p89

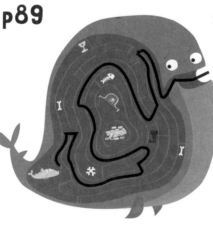

p90

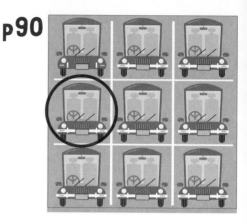

p91 - There are 29 children, so there is 1 space left for Mason.

p92 – Greensnot won with 15 fish.

p93 - Sun – sunglasses; rain – umbrella; wind – kite; snow – sled; fog – flashlight; ice – ice skates

p94

p95
1. PARIS
2. WASHINGTON
3. ROME
4. MOSCOW
5. LONDON
6. DUBLIN

p96 - 97

p98
1, 11	7, 10
2, 6	8, 19
3, 15	9, 17
4, 18	12, 16
5, 14	13, 20

p99

p100 - There are 30 outlines.

p101

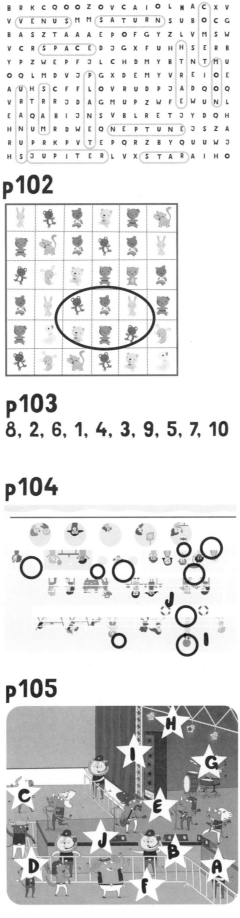

p102

p103
8, 2, 6, 1, 4, 3, 9, 5, 7, 10

p104

p105

p106-107 - There are 10 butterfly pairs.

p108
A–3	D–6
B–5	E–1
C–4	F–2

p109
ELEP-HANT	MON-KEY
GOR-ILLA	SCOR-PION
LI-ON	BO-AR
SK-UNK	VUL-TURE

p110   F, C, E, B, A, D

p111
1, E	5, A
2, G	6, B
3, F	7, D
4, H	8, C

p112 - Silhouette D

p113
duck	skunk
rat	spider
octopus	frog

p114

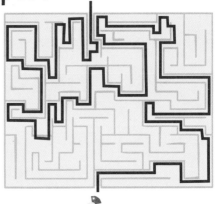

p115
Jenny has bike B
Alicia has bike **C**
Emily has bike A

p116

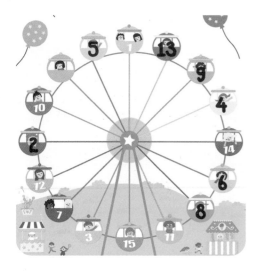

p117

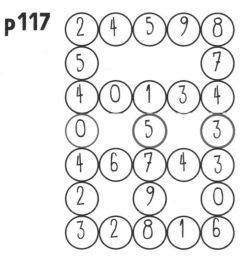

p118-119

p120 - Your dot-to-dot should reveal a crocodile!

TOTALLY AMAZING MAZES

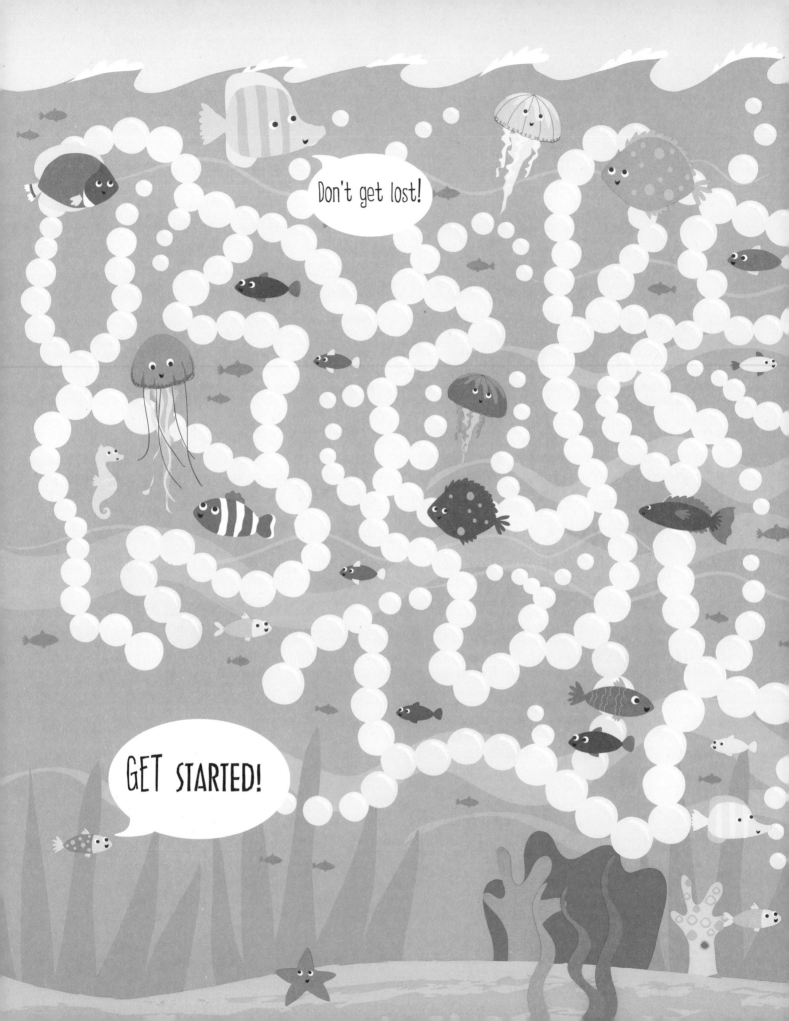

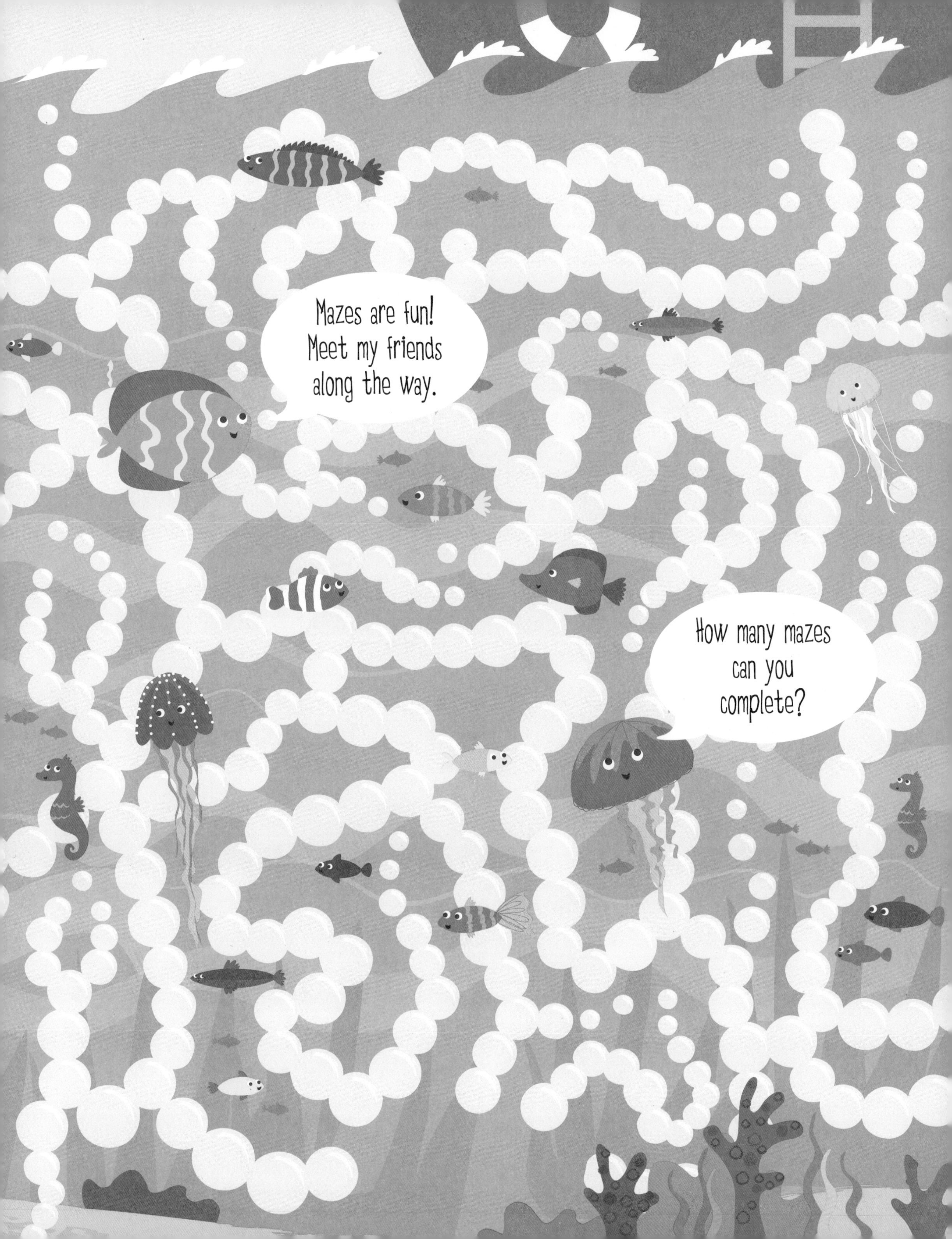
Mazes are fun! Meet my friends along the way.
How many mazes can you complete?

133

Help the zombie hunter find a route to catch all 10 escaped zombies, then return them to the graveyard.

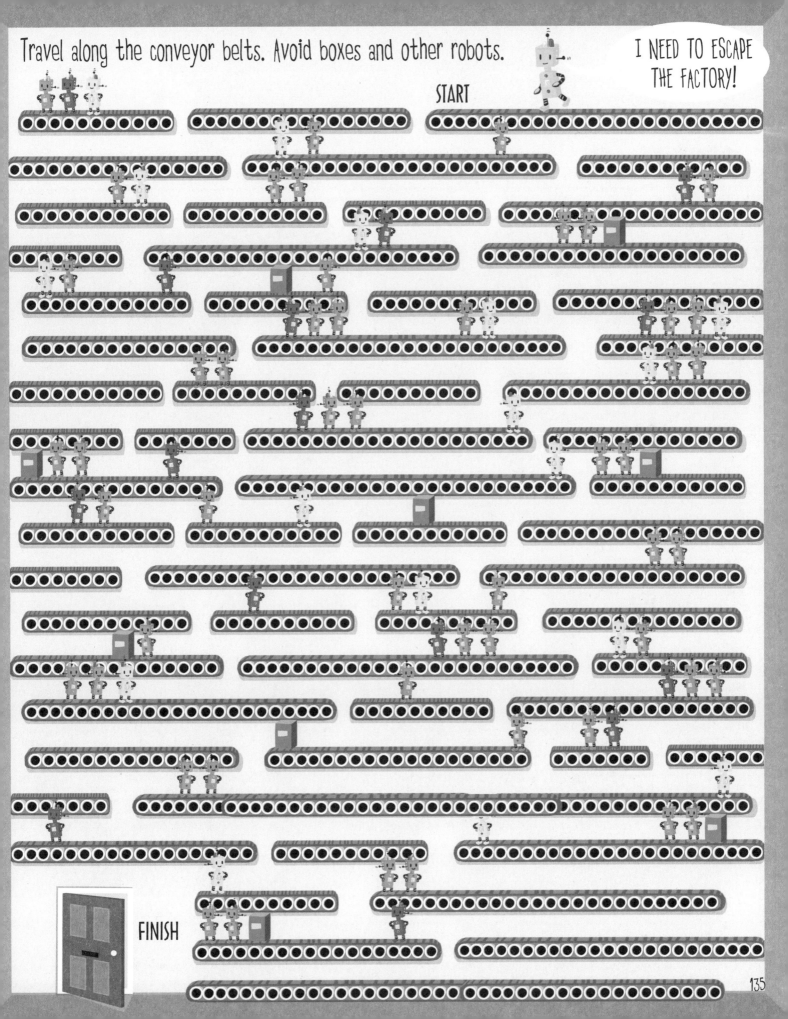

Travel along the conveyor belts. Avoid boxes and other robots.

I NEED TO ESCAPE THE FACTORY!

START

FINISH

Help Little Fish escape Octopus's tangly arms.

START

FINISH

137

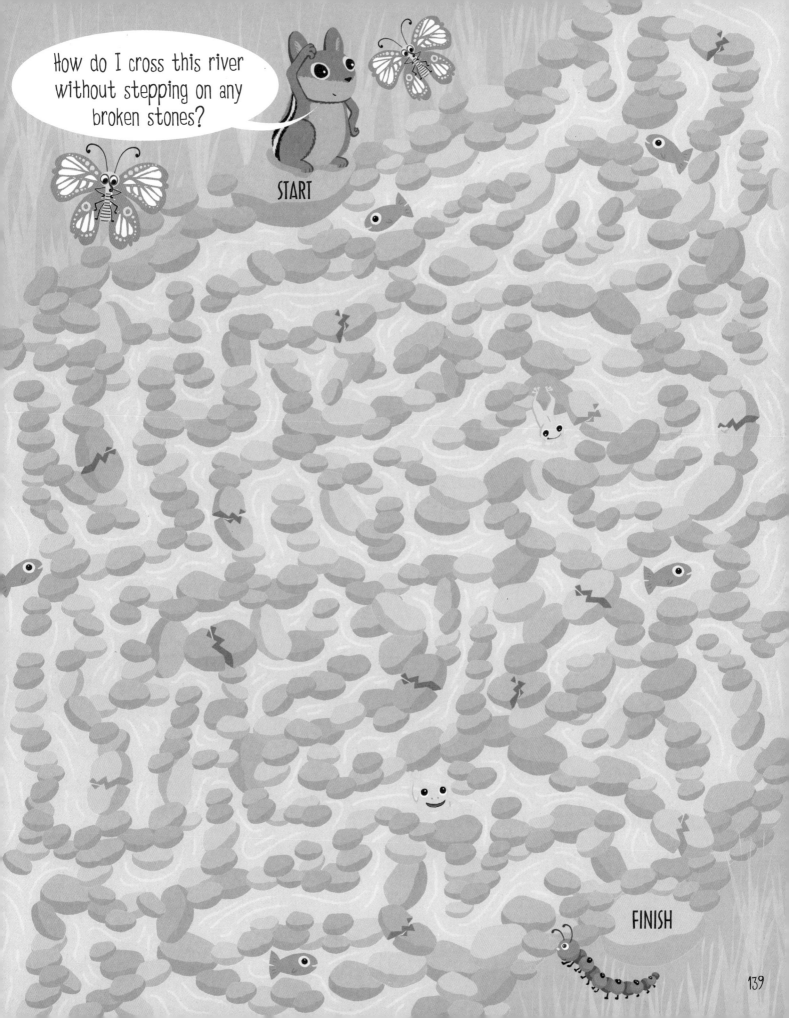

Help Ella find the way between the
umbrellas to her matching umbrella.

START

FINISH

Twelve teachers have been turned into monsters in a science experiment disaster. Collect the bottle of antidote from the science lab ... just don't bump into any monsters on the way!

START

FINISH

22+14

One of these star trails will lead us to planet Earth.

START

FINISH

This car isn't ready to be crushed. Drive it out of the wrecking yard.

START

FINISH

147

Meet Stunt Pilot Penguin, about to perform another death-defying trick. Follow the vapor trails to land him safely.

START

Way to go,
Stunt Pilot Penguin!

FINISH

149

Take a tour of Thrillville Theme Park.

START

150

FINISH

Help the caterpillar munch its way along
a trail of leaves to its friend.

START

FINISH

Use the empty ladders to get Roofer Rob to the leaky roof.

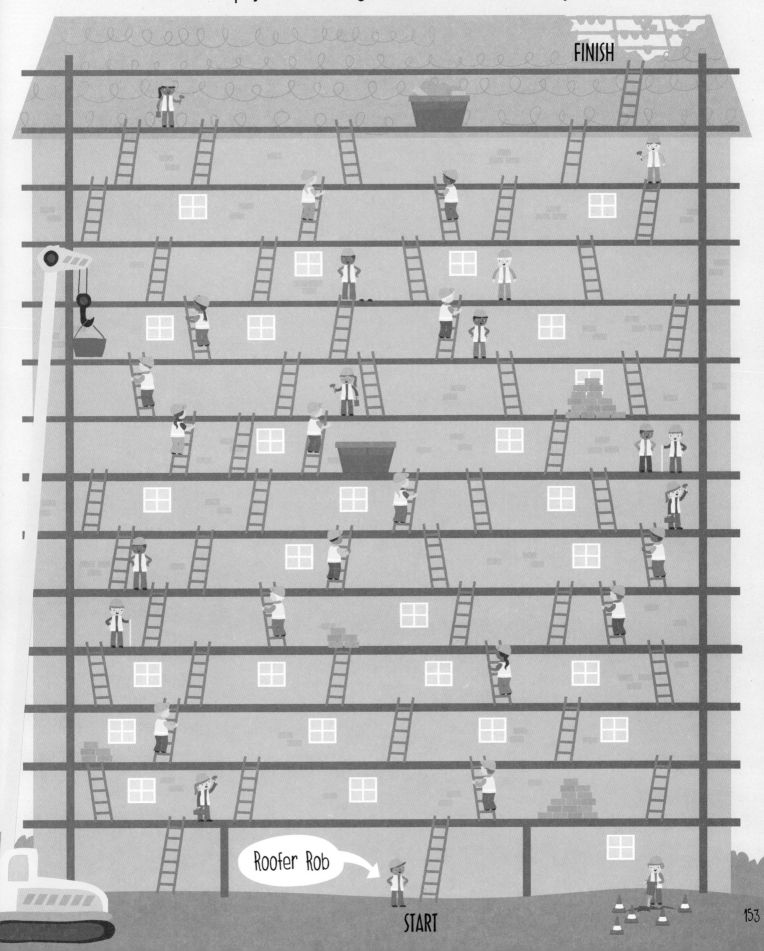

FINISH

Roofer Rob

START

153

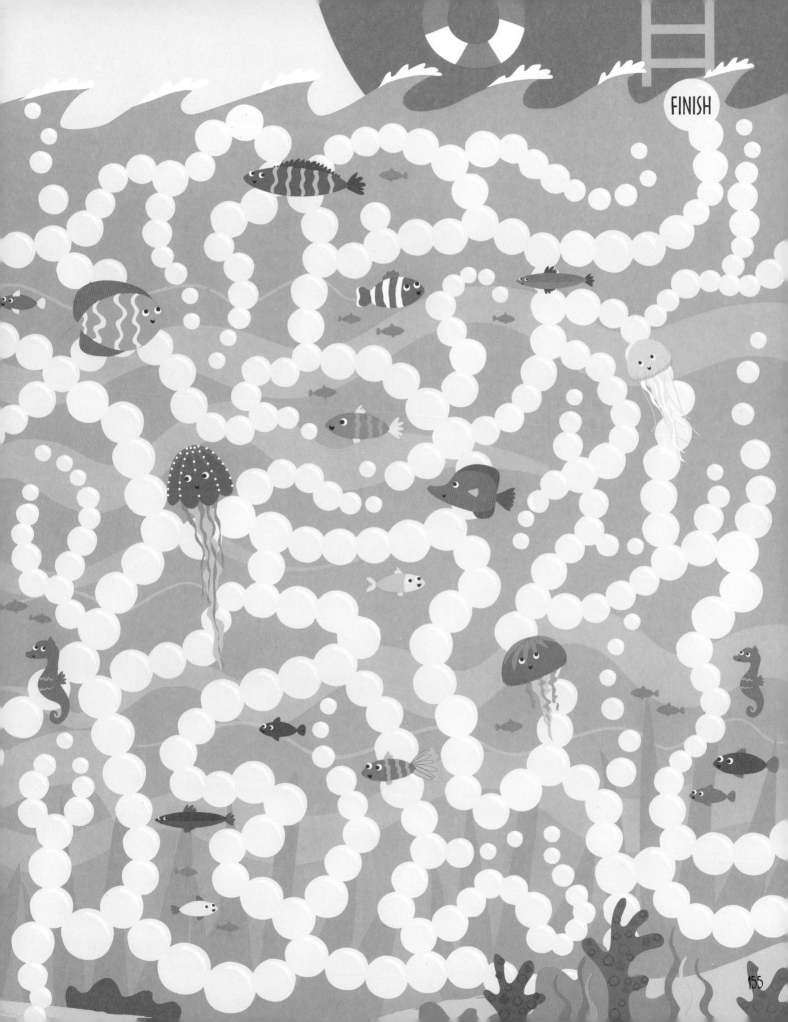

FINISH

155

Slimy wants to meet Shelly for lunch. Help him avoid all the creepy-crawlies on the way.

START

FINISH

Take the escaped mummy back to where it belongs.
Don't scare any tourists on the way!

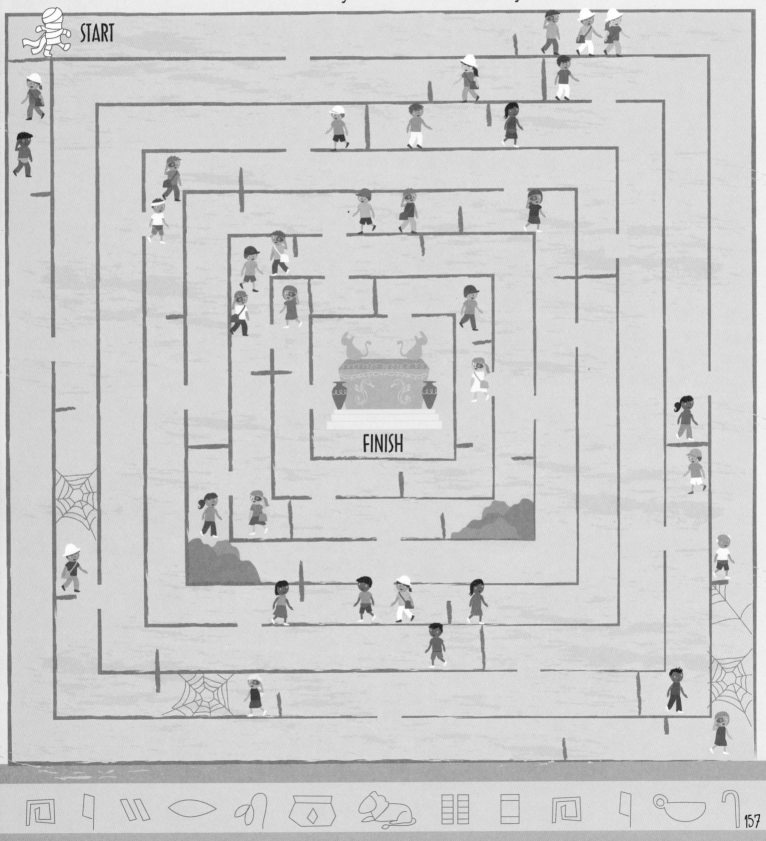

START

FINISH

Avoid the knots in this sneaker tangle!

START

FINISH

Quick, you've got a plane to catch! Jump in this taxi to the airport.
Don't run any red lights along the way.

START

FINISH

162

Race the mouse to the attic and get through the mouse hole to escape the cat. Use stairs, ladders, and open doors to get there.

FINISH

START

163

FINISH

START

WATCH OUT
FOR DEADLY
RATTLESNAKES!

Carefully climb Cactus Canyon ...

165

Deep in the jungle, the explorers are hoping to catch sight of the rare giant panda. Travel between the bamboo branches.

START

FINISH

167

FINISH

START

This ticket lets me jump past all these people to the front of the line!

168

Ride the rollercoaster. Just avoid the other cars!

START

FINISH

Can you smell toasting marshmallows? Find your way to the campfire.

START

FINISH

Follow the snow trails. There's only one way down!

START

FINISH

171

FINISH

173

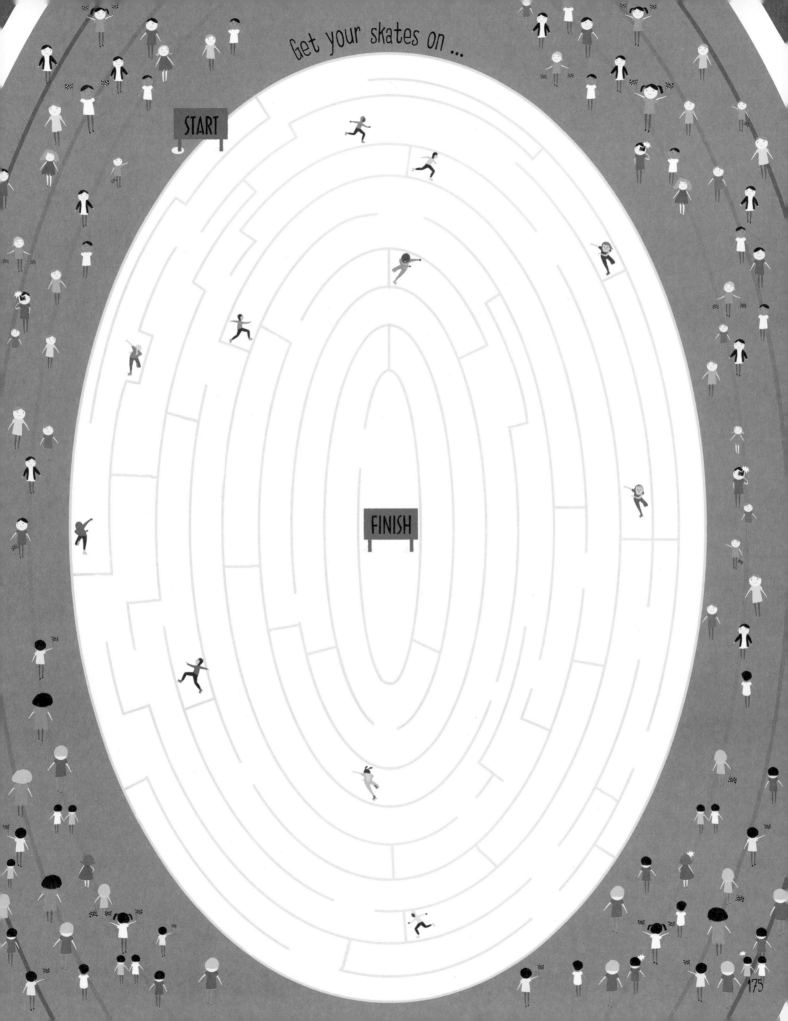

Get your skates on ...

START

FINISH

FINISH

START

Unlock the safe to get your hands on the world's largest diamond.

Loop between the popsicles for a sweet reward!

START

FINISH

177

Nee-nah! Nee-nah! Drive the fire crew to the rescue!

START

178

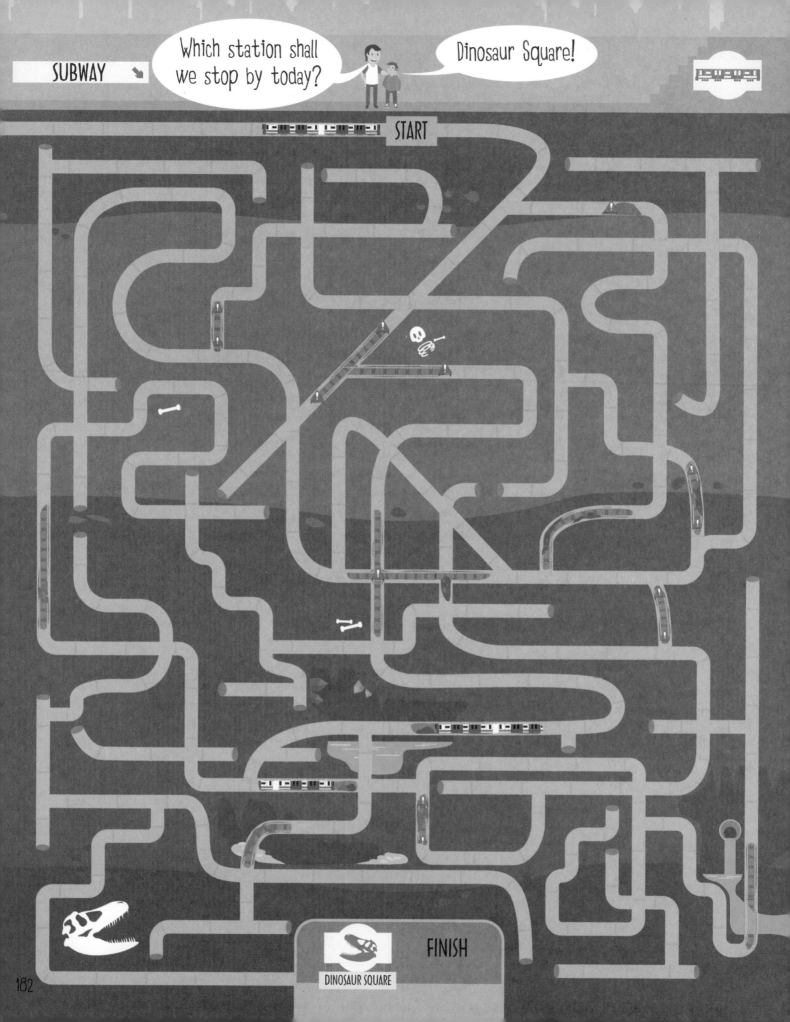

Guide Curtis the cat through the streets to his friends.

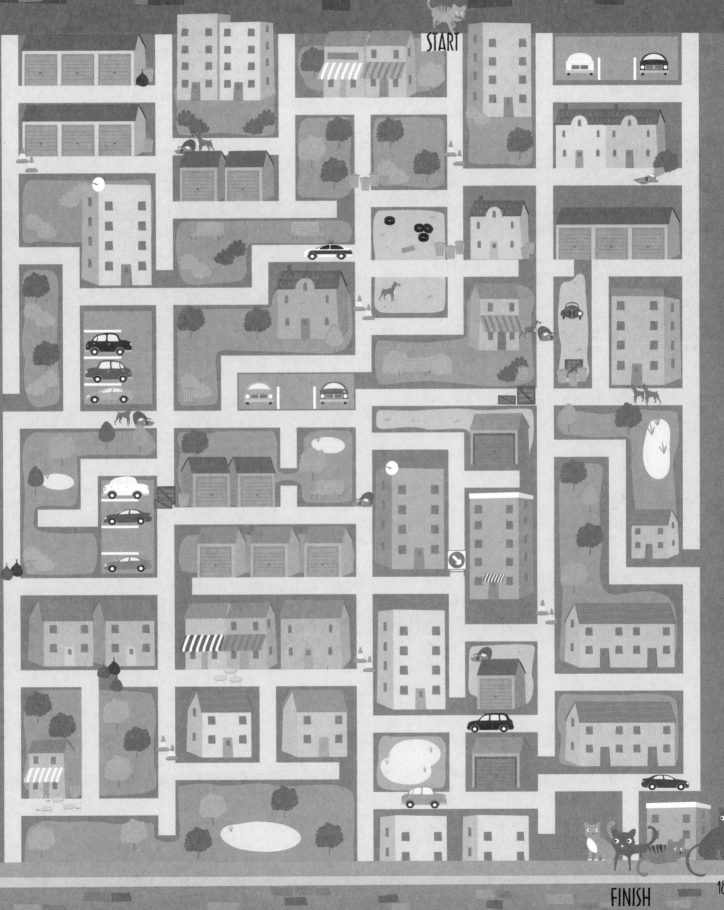

START

FINISH

Princess Polly wants to climb the tower and see the WHOLE kingdom.

The view's great up here!

FINISH

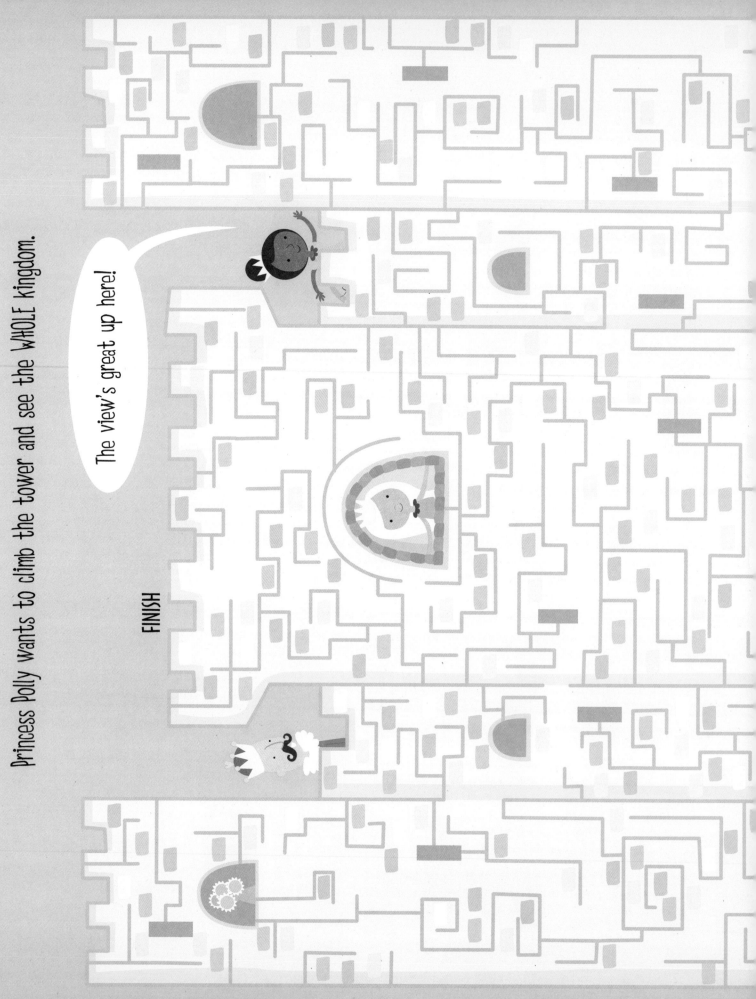

START

How do I get to the tower?

Guide the seahorse between the seaweed to his true love.

START

FINISH

187

The intrepid archaeologist has found an ancient Aztec ruin in the jungle.
Who knows what treasure he might find in the temple ... if he can get there!

FINISH

Where did I
put that map?

START

REALLY BRAVE

FINISH

TOTALLY AWESOME!

GETTING BRAVER

BEGINNER

START

Take the ski lift to the highest mountain.
You can only travel along cables
without another car on them.

191

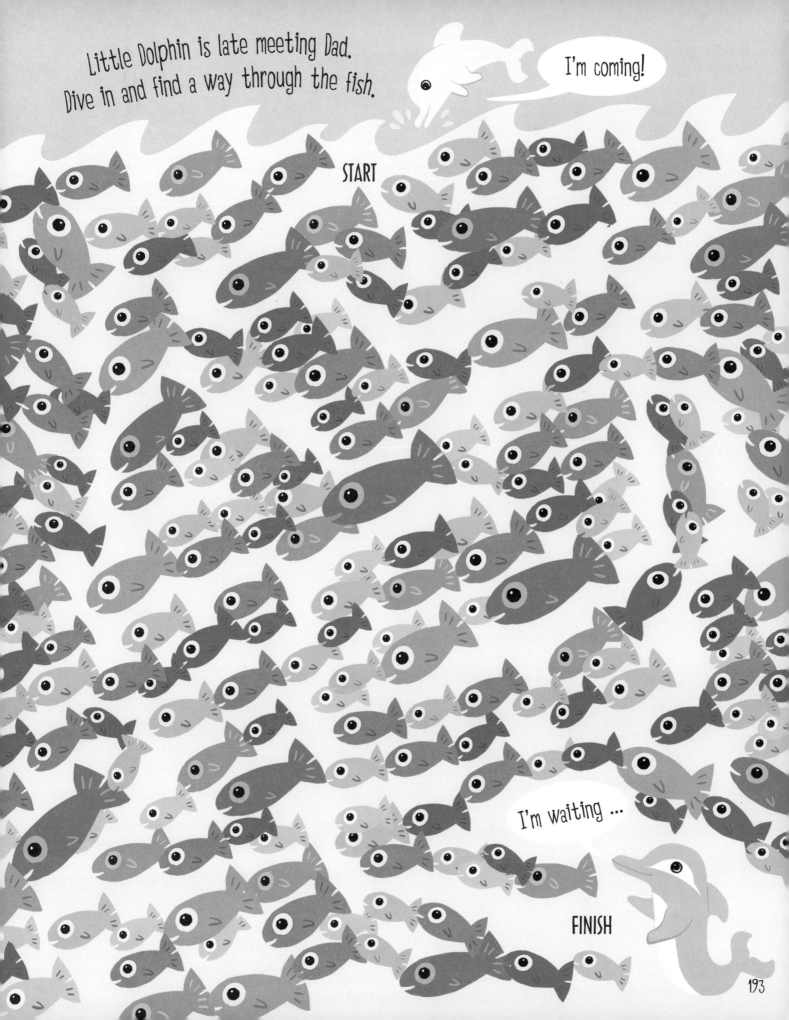

Travel over each blue ghost to zap them all on the way to the end of the level.

FINISH

START

Baby Bird has taken her
first flight, but can't fly back
up to the nest. Help her hop
back up the branches.

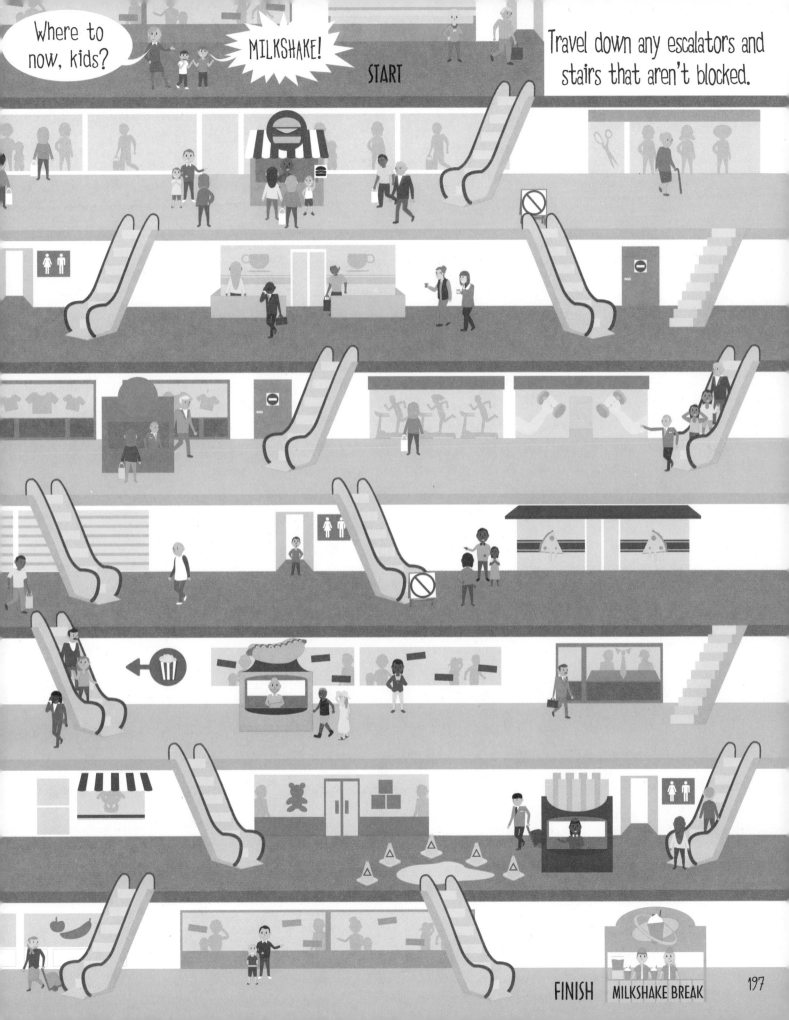

START

Go, Mia!

Just one lap to go ... Mia can still win the race! Avoid the other drivers and race to the finish.

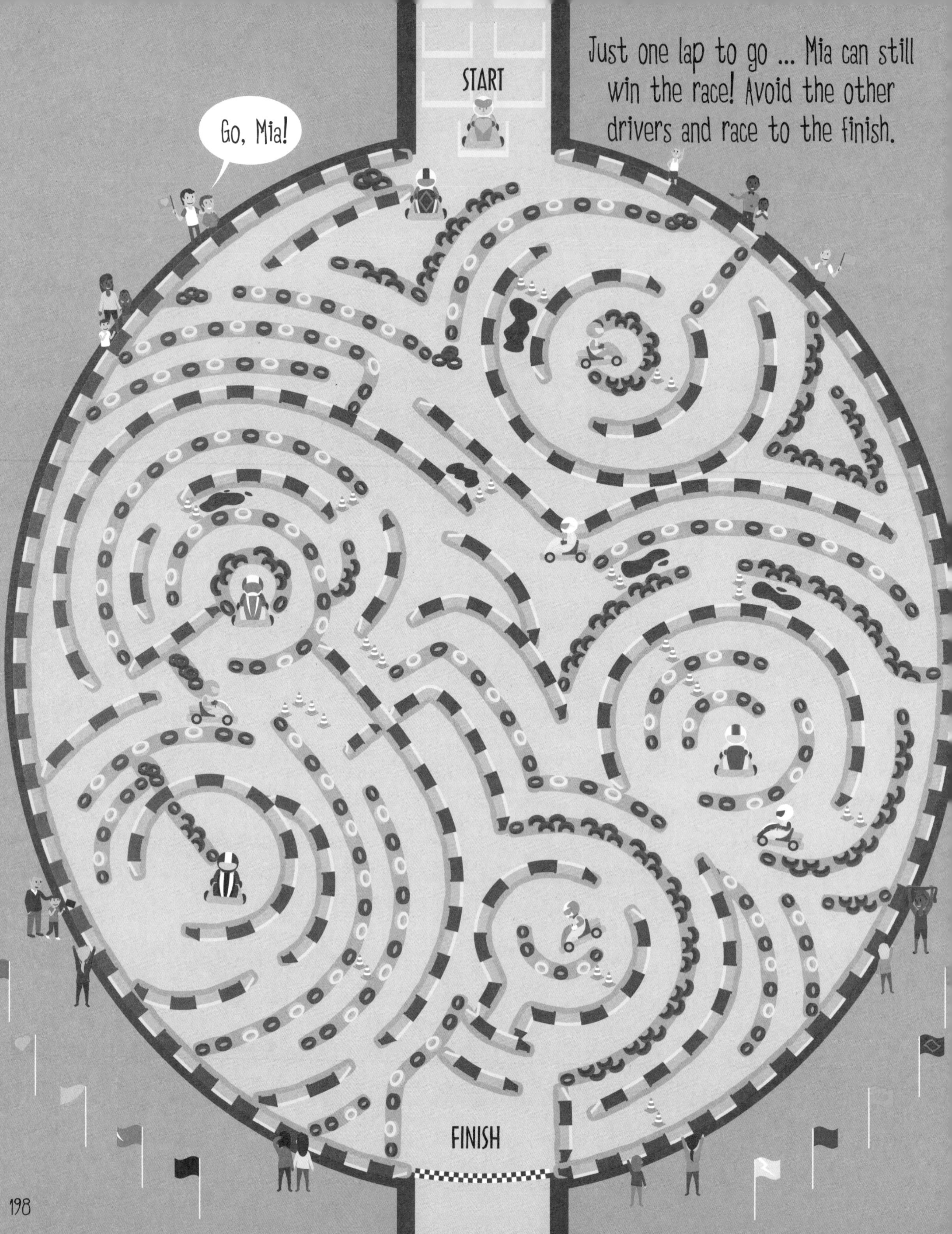

FINISH

Edge through the hedges to the magical fountain.

START

FINISH

199

Help Alice follow the tangle of dog leashes to the ice cream van to find her pooch!

START

FINISH

201

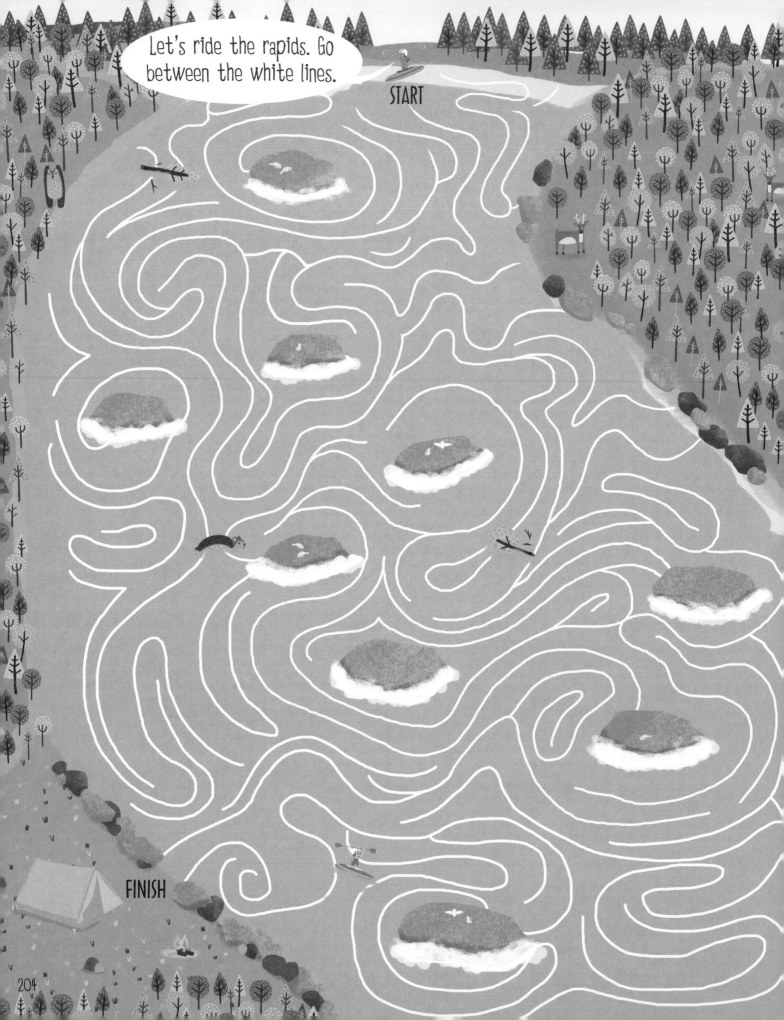

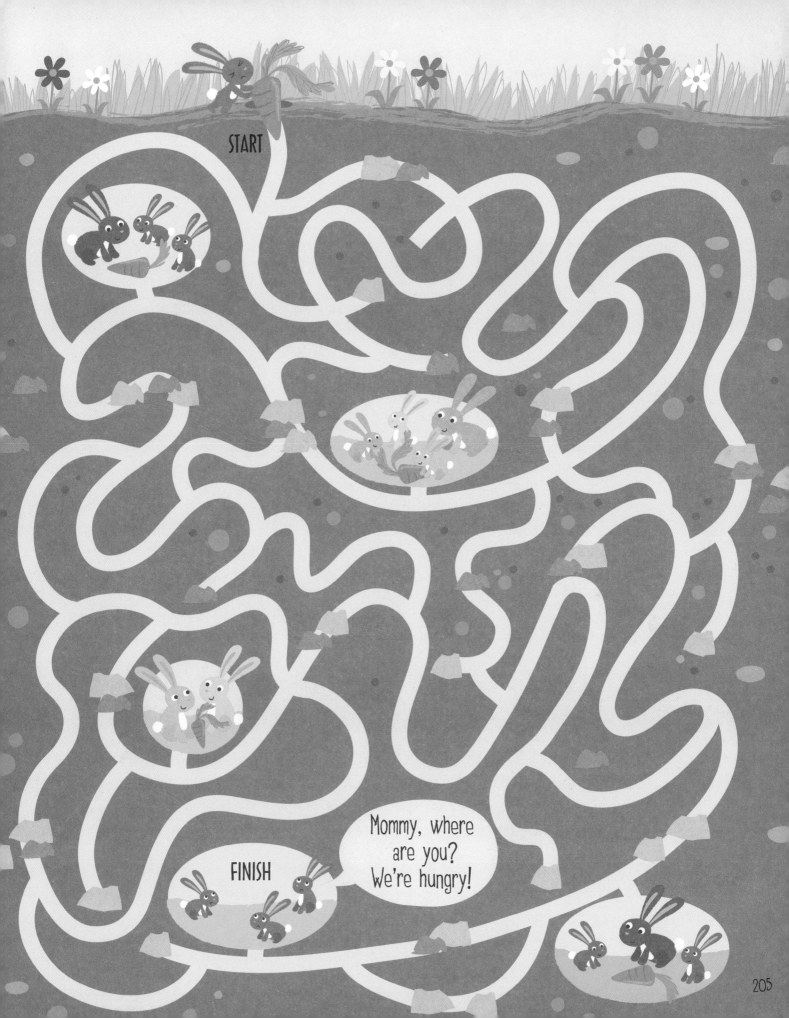

Seal feeding starts soon. If you're really quick, you can visit the tigers, zebras, shark, and raccoons on the way!

SEAL FEEDING AT 2PM

START

FINISH

208

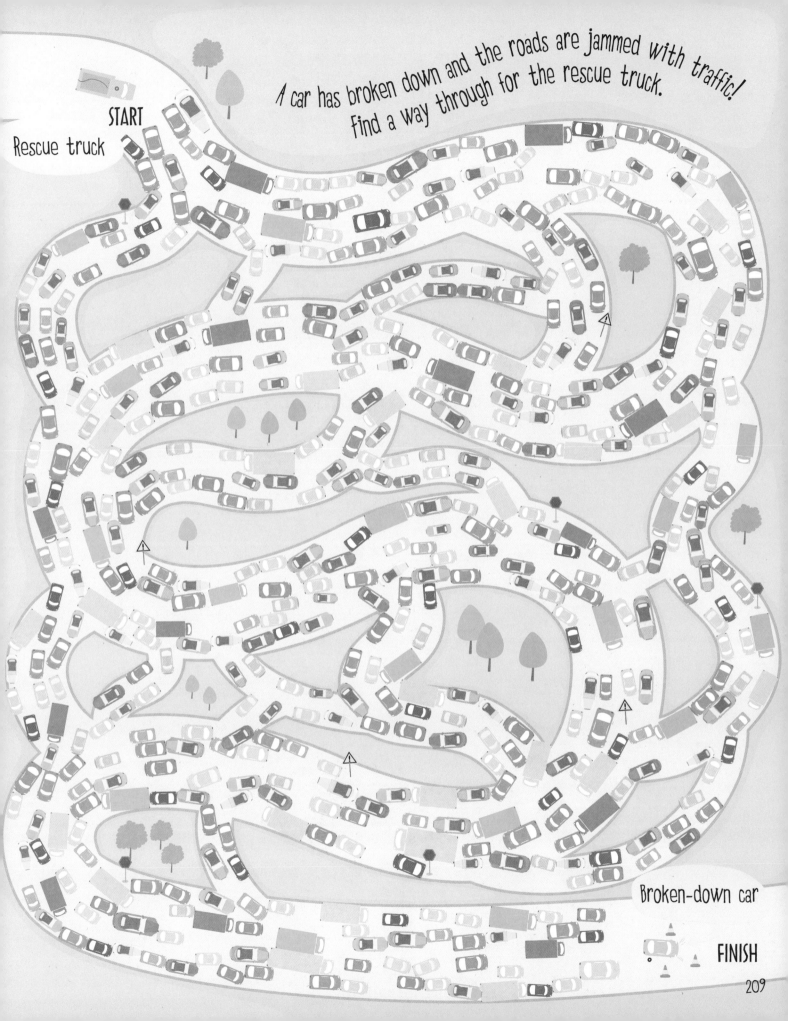

START
Rescue truck

A car has broken down and the roads are jammed with traffic!
Find a way through for the rescue truck.

Broken-down car

FINISH

209

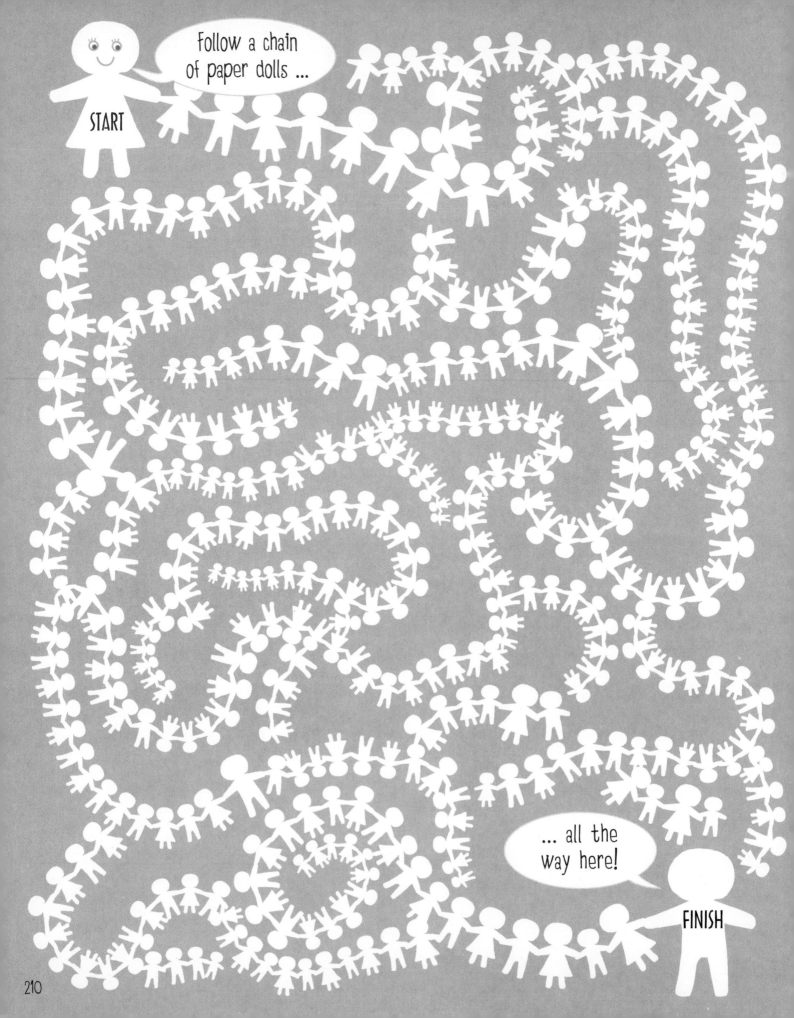

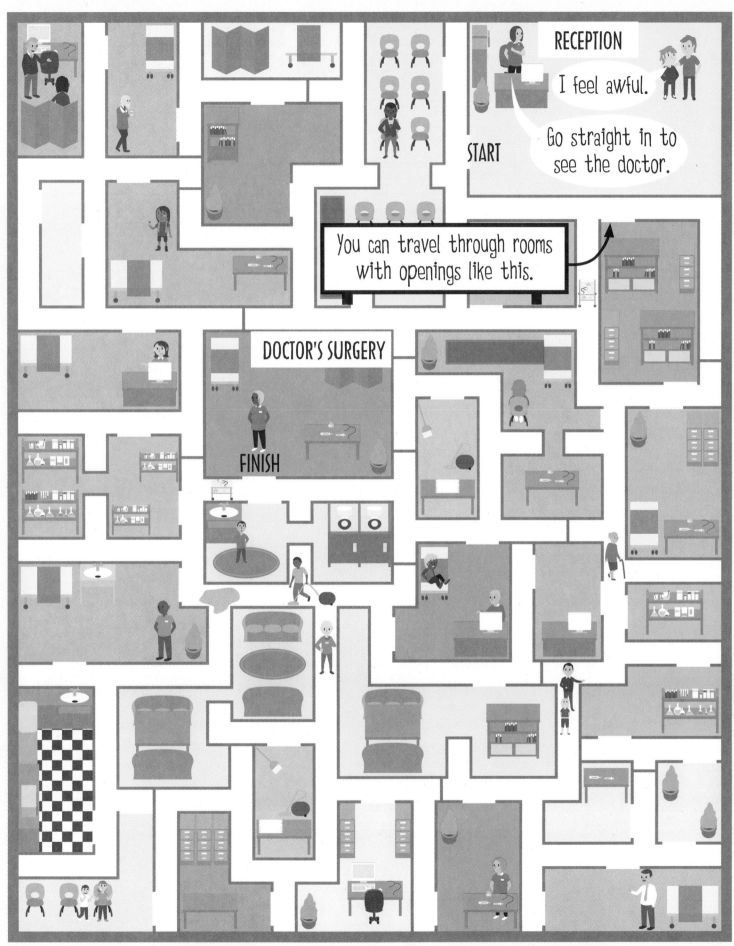

211

Monkey has lost his troop ...

START ➔

212

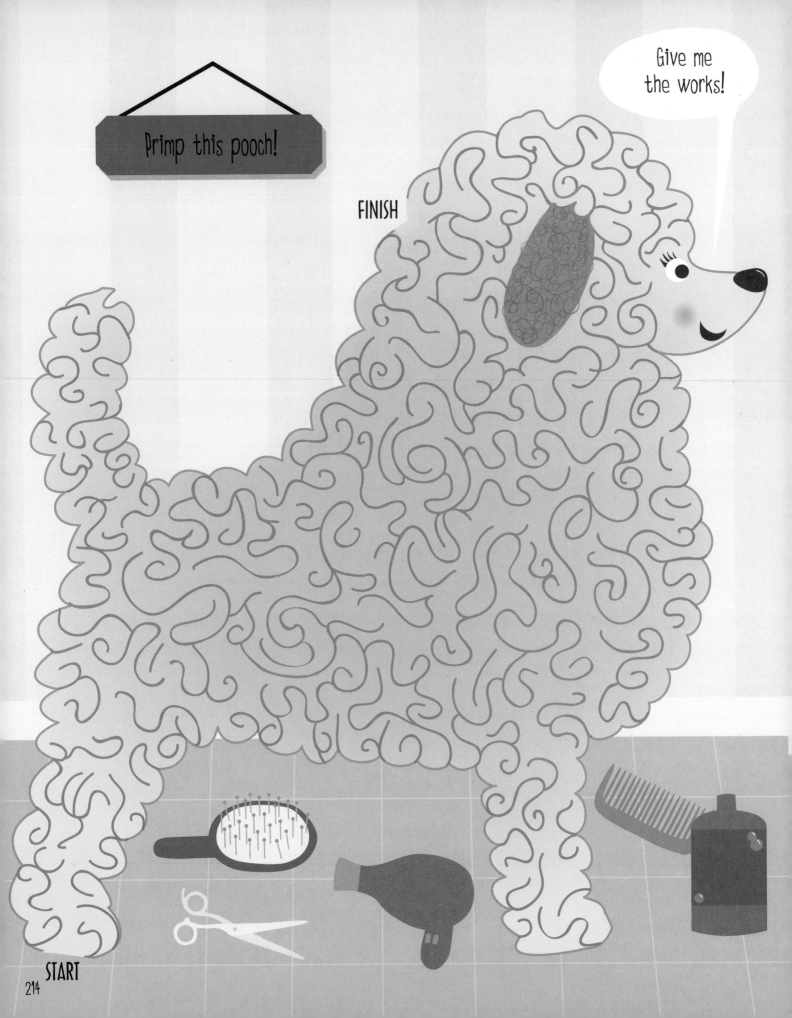

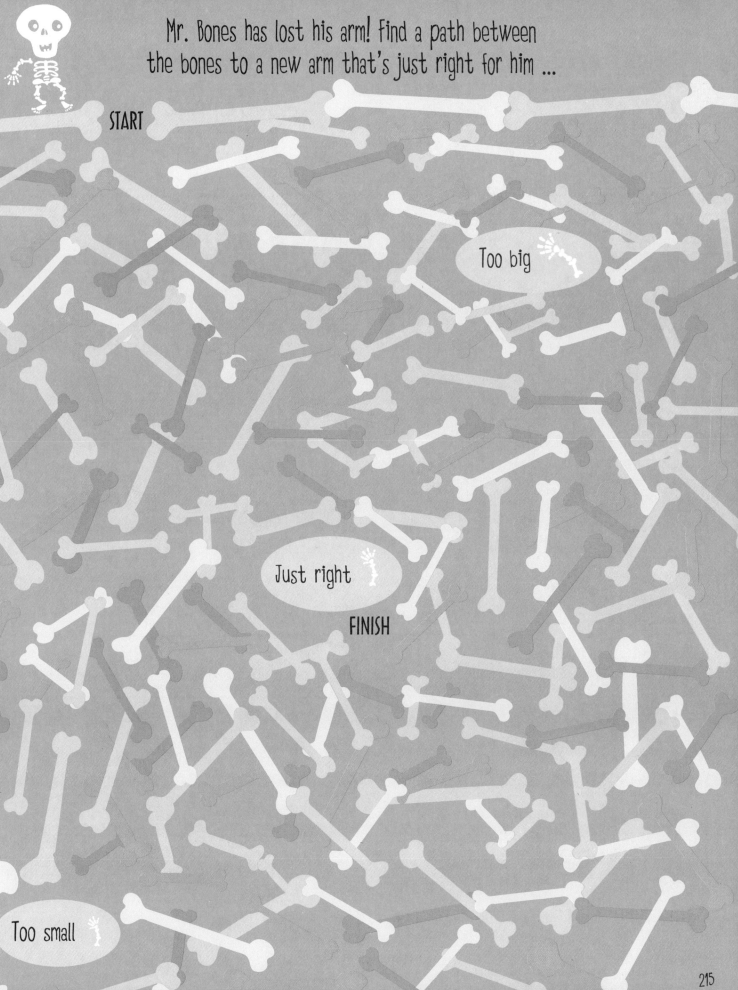

Mr. Bones has lost his arm! Find a path between
the bones to a new arm that's just right for him ...

START

Too big

Just right

FINISH

Too small

215

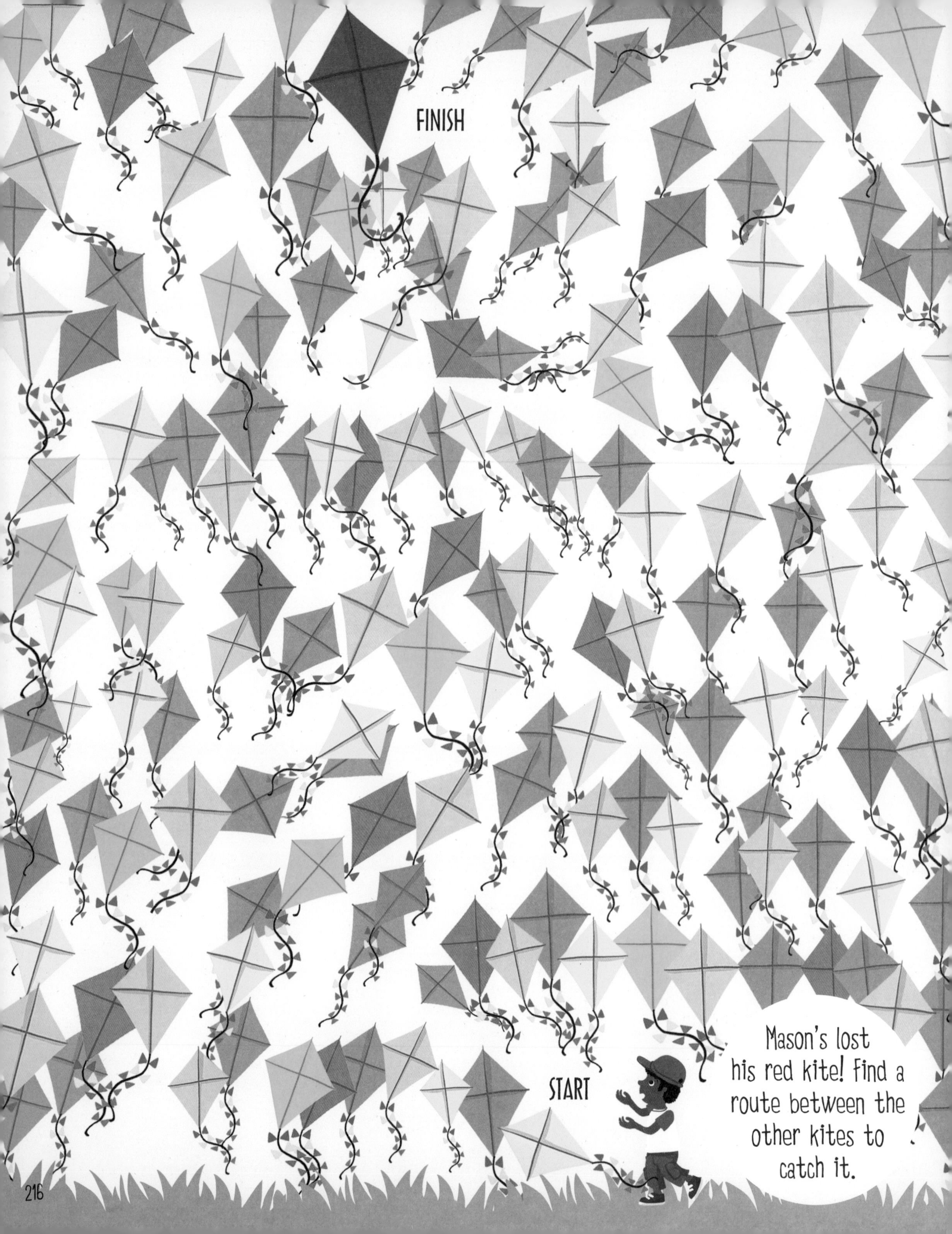

FINISH

START

Mason's lost
his red kite! Find a
route between the
other kites to
catch it.

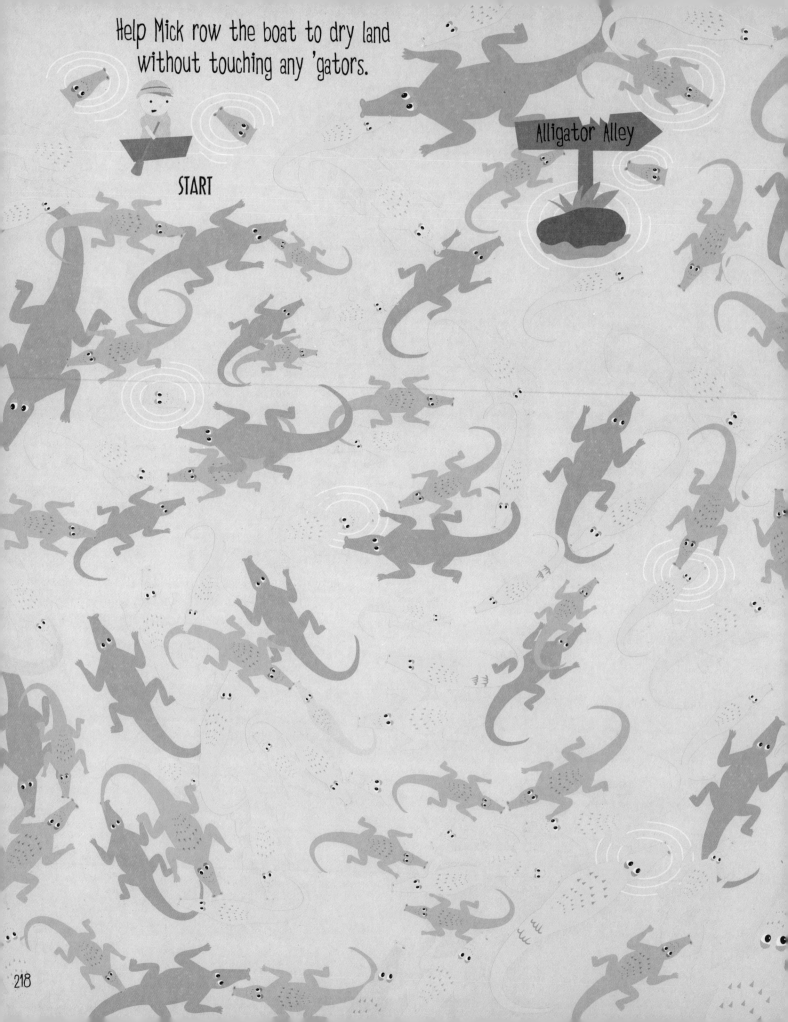

Help Mick row the boat to dry land without touching any 'gators.

START

Alligator Alley

FINISH

219

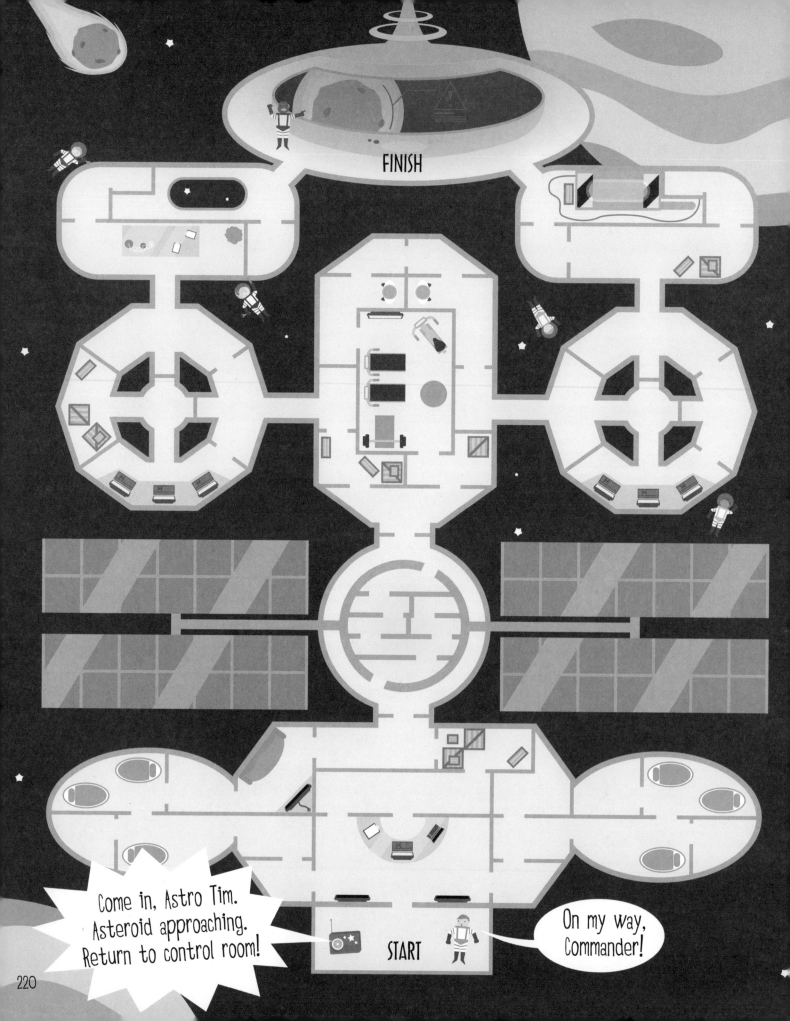

Ellie has lost her daddy in the herd. Help her find a route between the other elephants to be reunited with him.

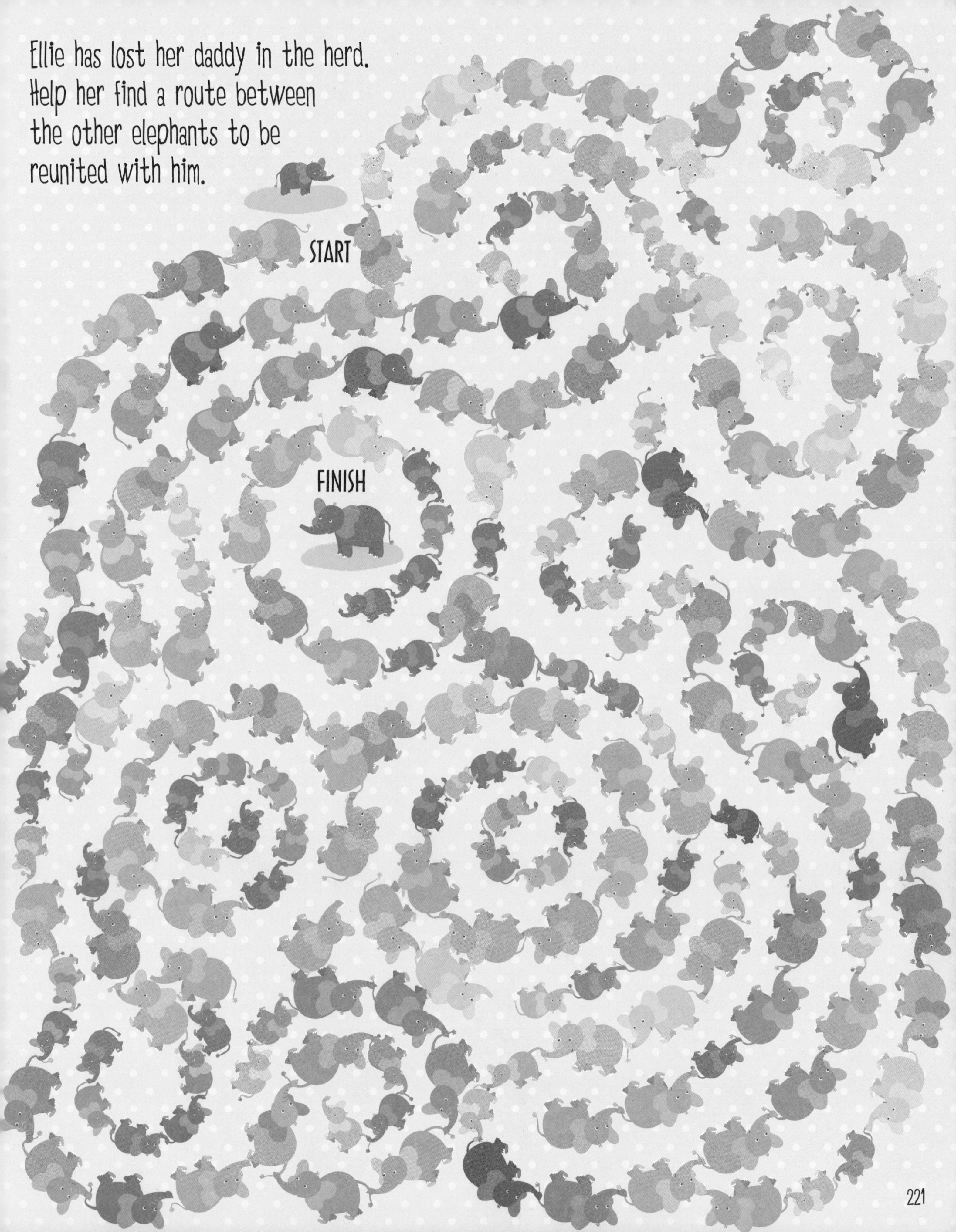

START

FINISH

START

Ben's only got ten minutes left in the Adventure Play Park. Pass every red flag to visit each activity and get him to the exit ... Mom's waiting!

FINISH

START

FINISH

Help One-eyed Violet hop across the pirate ships to reach the treasure.

START

FINISH

224

As long as the bus driver picks up all six children on the way to school, everyone will be on time for class.

START

SCHOOL

FINISH

225

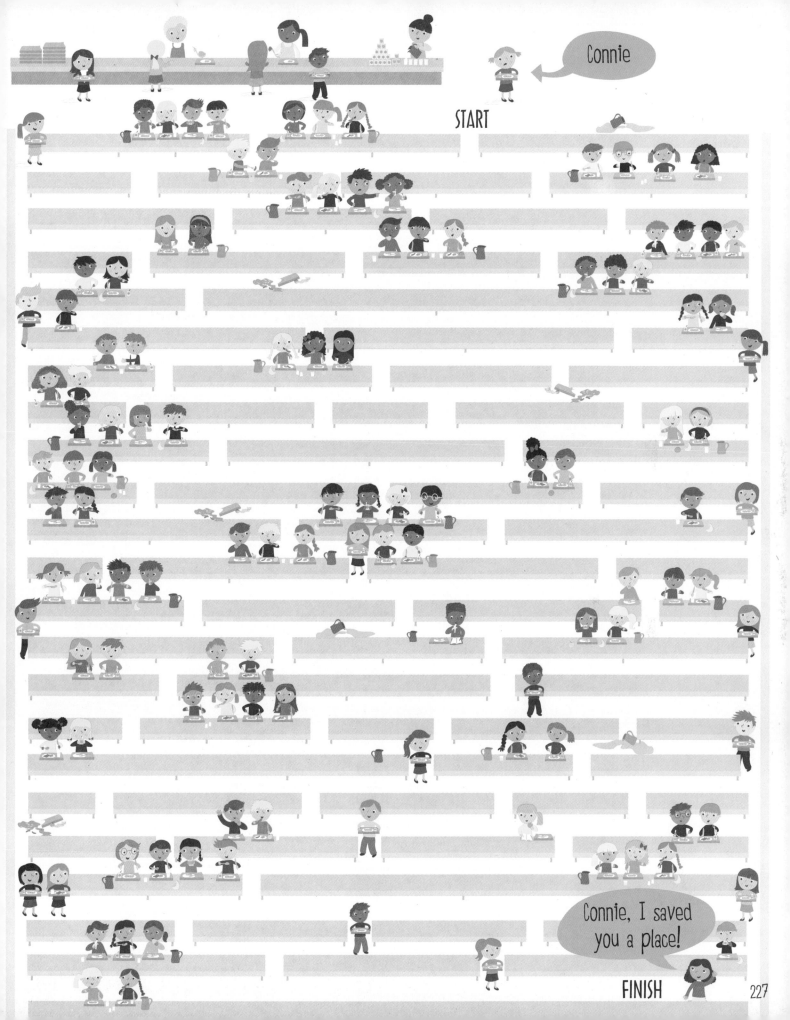

Connie

START

Connie, I saved you a place!

FINISH

227

START

Avoid the seaweed tangle
and guide Marissa the mermaid home.

HOME

FINISH

228

229

It's the rally in the valley!
Skid 'n' slide to the finish line.

START

FINISH

230

231

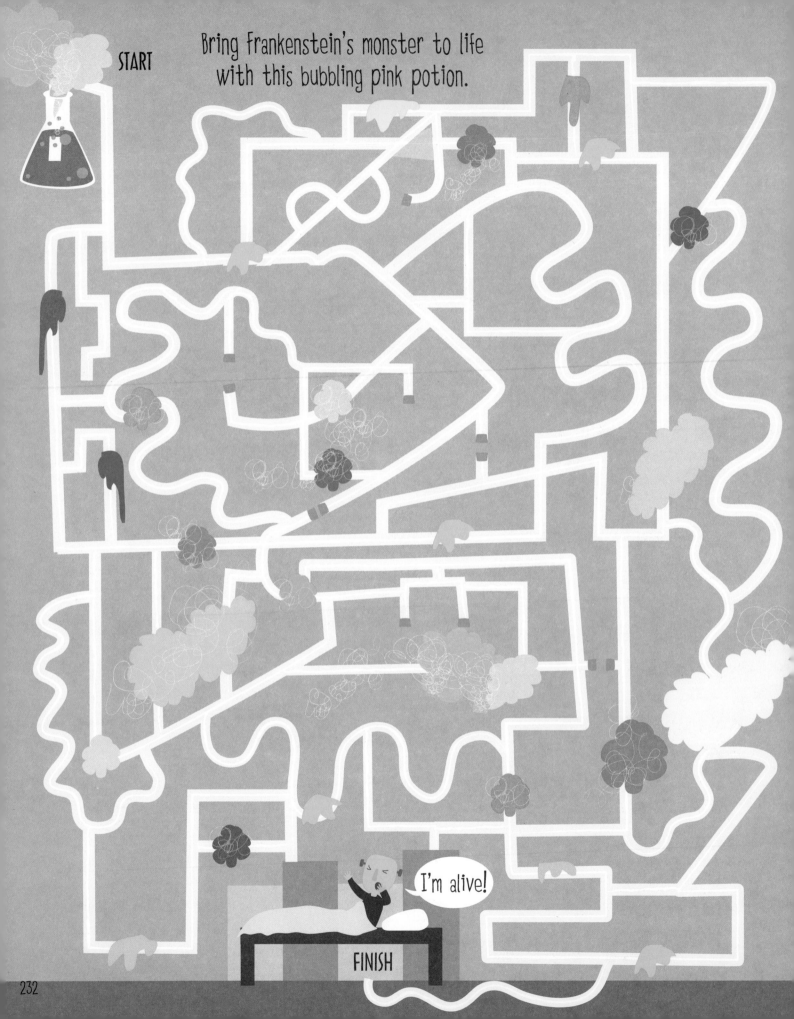

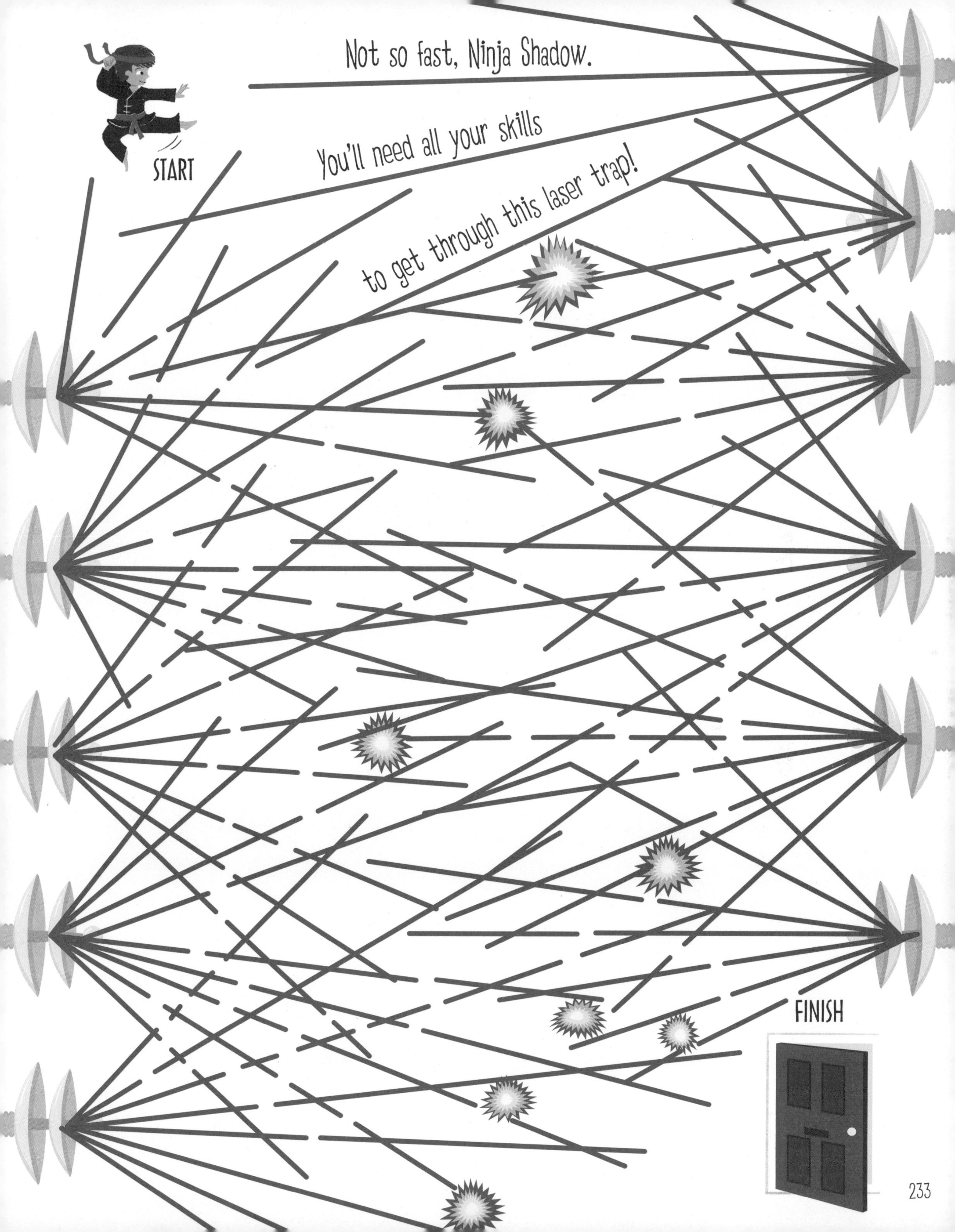

START

Not so fast, Ninja Shadow.

You'll need all your skills

to get through this laser trap!

FINISH

Make the most of your safari trip and see every animal along the way!
Watch out for other safari vehicles.

START

FINISH

235

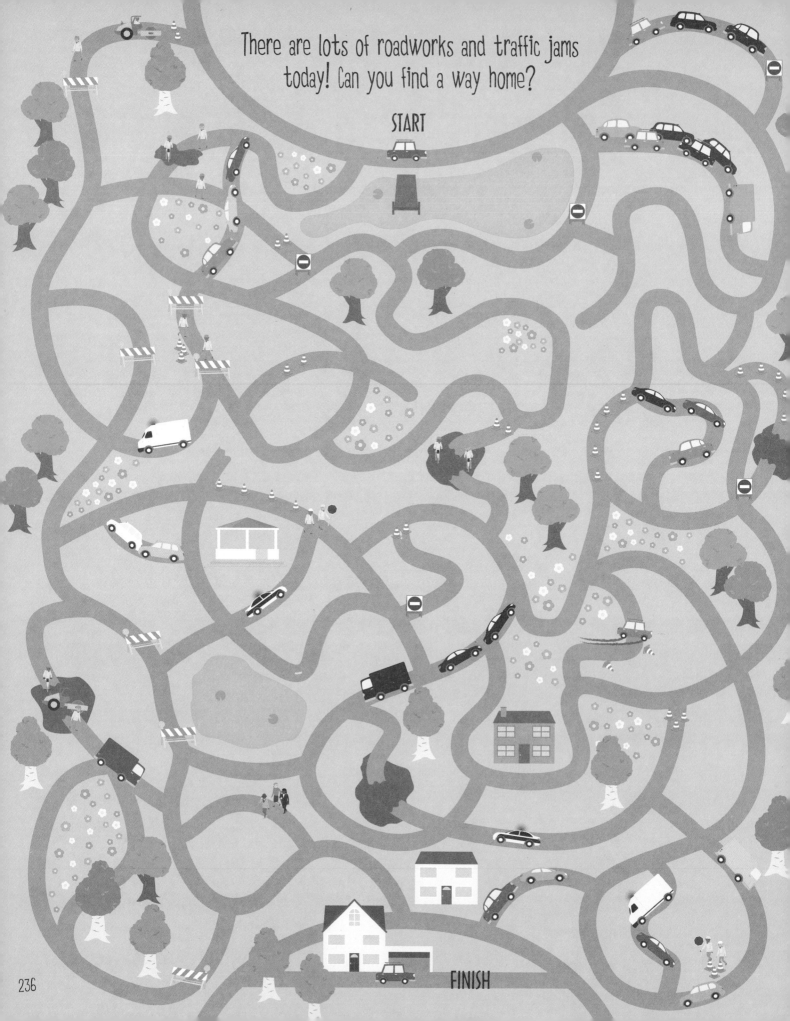

There are lots of roadworks and traffic jams today! Can you find a way home?

START

FINISH

Mega Blob and his beastly buddies are taking over the city.
There's only one thing for it ... RUN!

START

FINISH

238

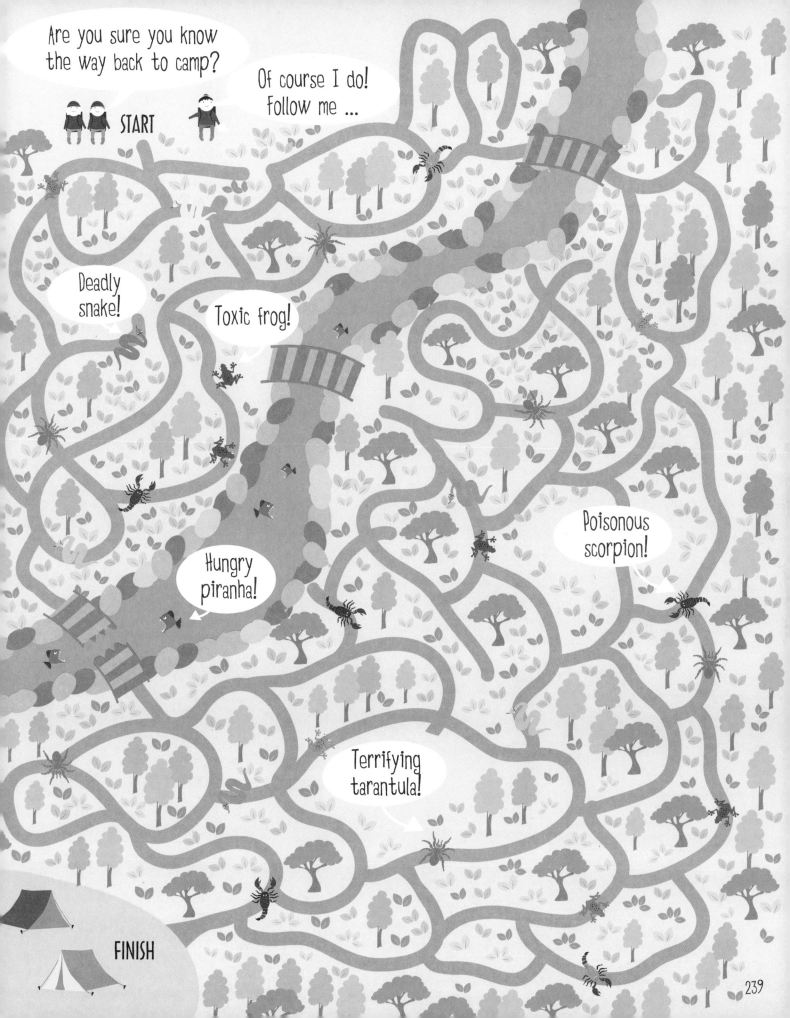

240

FINISH

Help Danny find the eraser in his backpack.

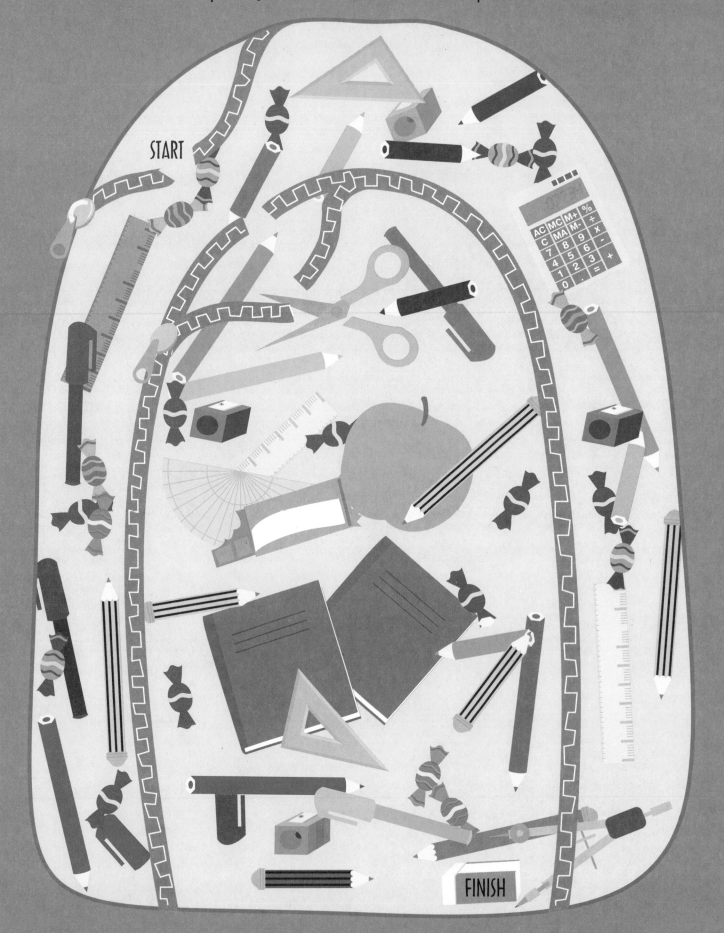

START

FINISH

Help the woodsman find his log piles.
He's going home to build a toasty fire!

START

FINISH

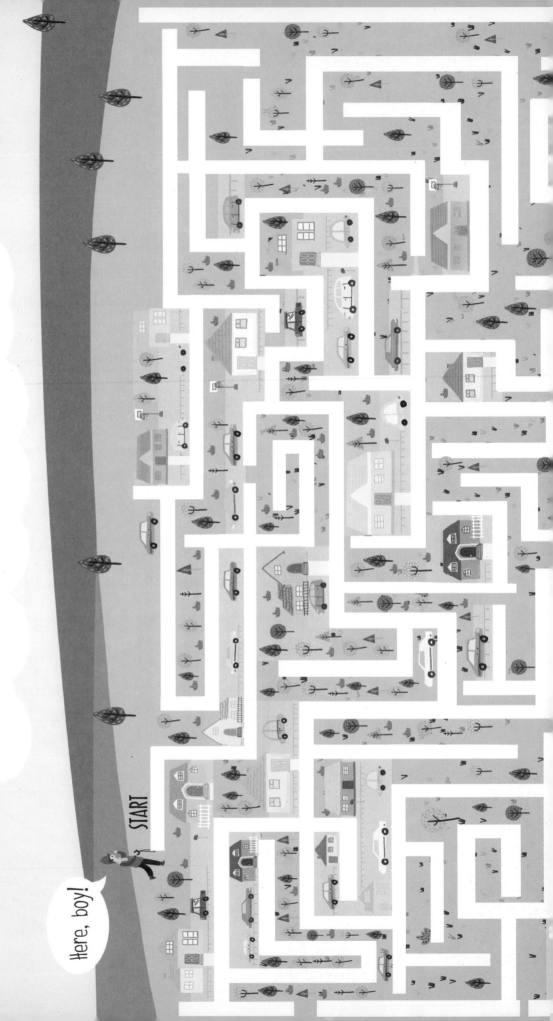

Fido has escaped (again). Can you help his owner find him?

Here, boy!

START

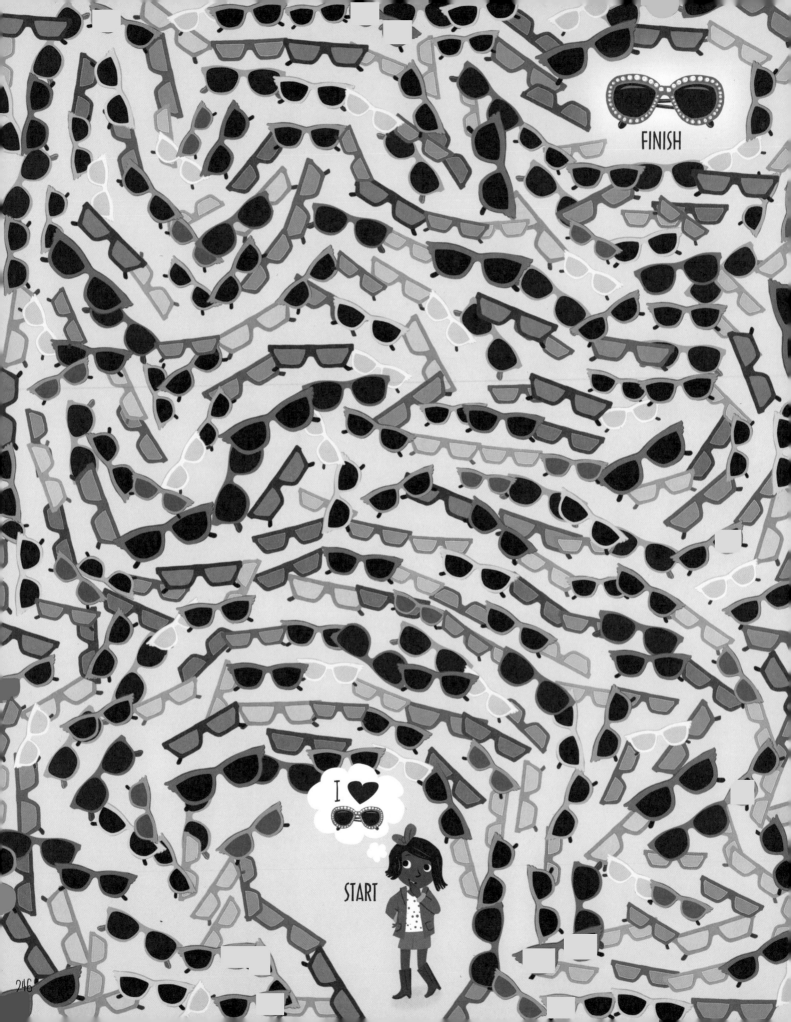

FINISH

I ♥

START

246

FINISH

START

Are the elevators not working?

Out of order

Out of order

Out of order

Never mind, Mrs. Director, you can take the stairs instead ... 247

FINISH

249

SOLUTIONS

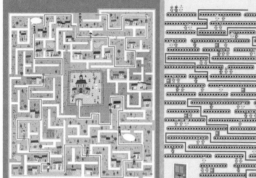

Page 134

Page 135

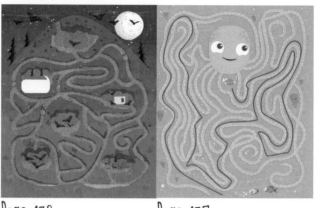

Page 136

Page 137

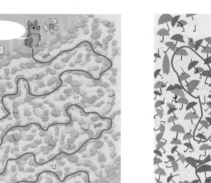

Page 138

Page 139

Pages 140-141

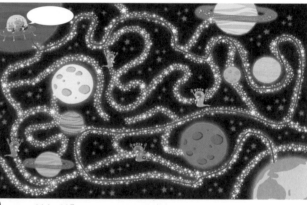

Page 142

Page 143

Pages 144-145

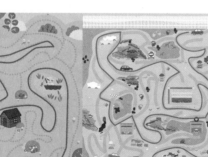

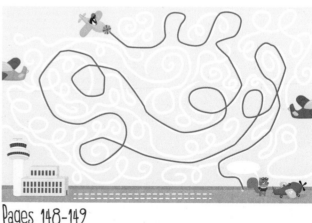

Page 146

Page 147

Pages 148-149

Pages 150-151

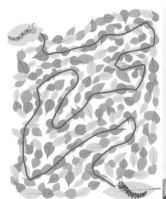
Page 152

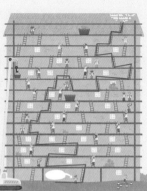
Page 153

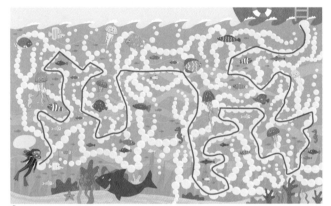
Pages 154-155

Page 156

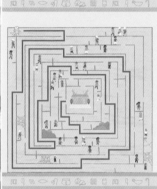
Page 157

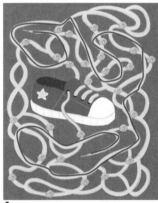
Page 158

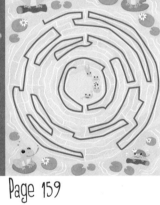
Page 159

Pages 160-161

Page 162

Page 163

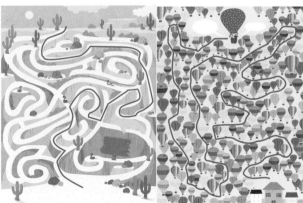
Page 164

Page 165

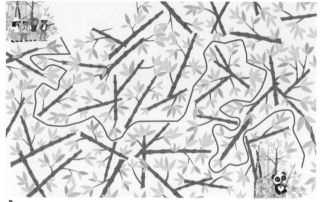

Pages 166-167

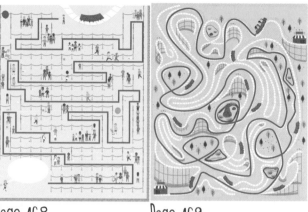

Page 168

Page 169

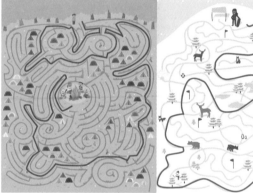

Page 170

Page 171

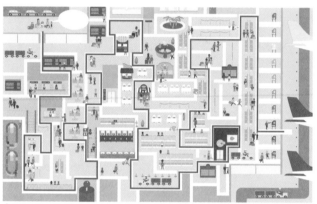

Pages 172-173

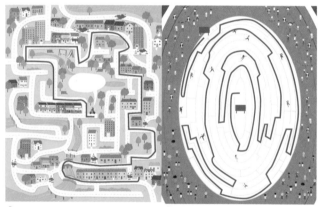

Page 174

Page 175

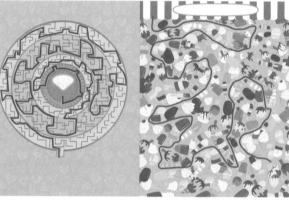

Page 176

Page 177

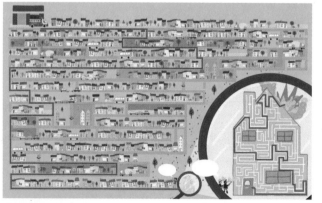

Pages 178-179

Page 180

Page 181

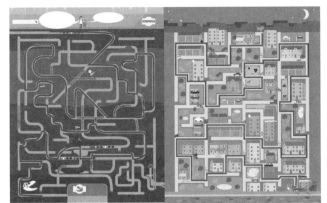

Page 182

Page 183

Pages 184-185

Page 186

Page 187

Page 188

Page 189

Page 190

Page 191

Page 192

Page 193

Page 194

Page 195

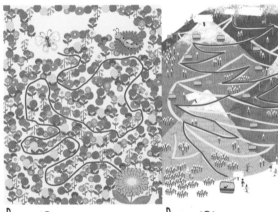

Page 196

Page 197

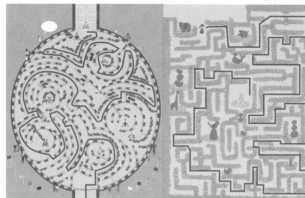

Page 198

Page 199

Page 200

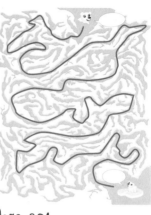

Page 201

Page 202

Page 203

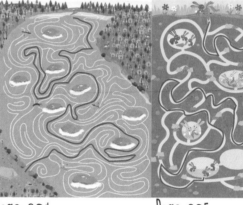

Page 204

Page 205

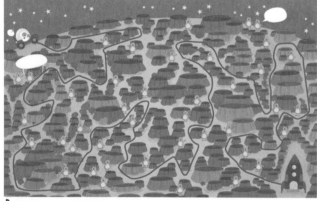

Pages 206-207

Page 208

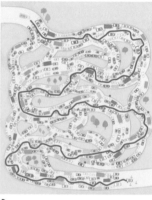

Page 209

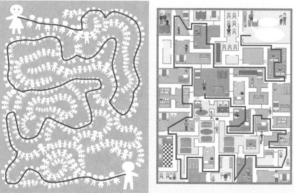

Page 210

Page 211

Pages 212-213

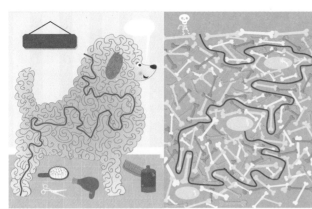

Page 214

Page 215

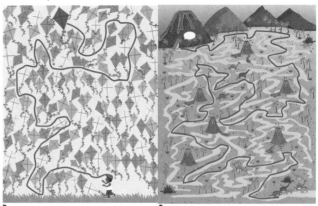

Page 216

Page 217

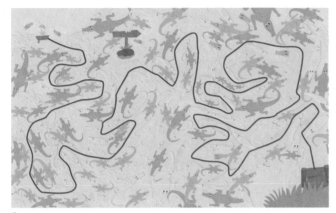

Pages 218-219

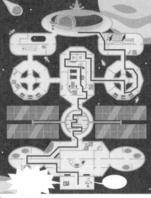

Page 220

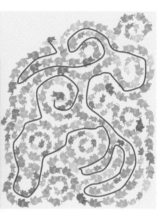

Page 221

Page 222

Page 223

Page 224

Page 225

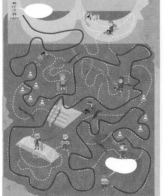

Page 226

Page 227

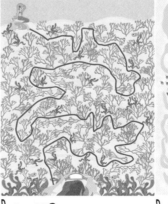

Page 228

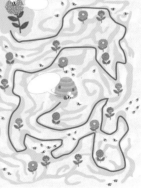

Page 229

255

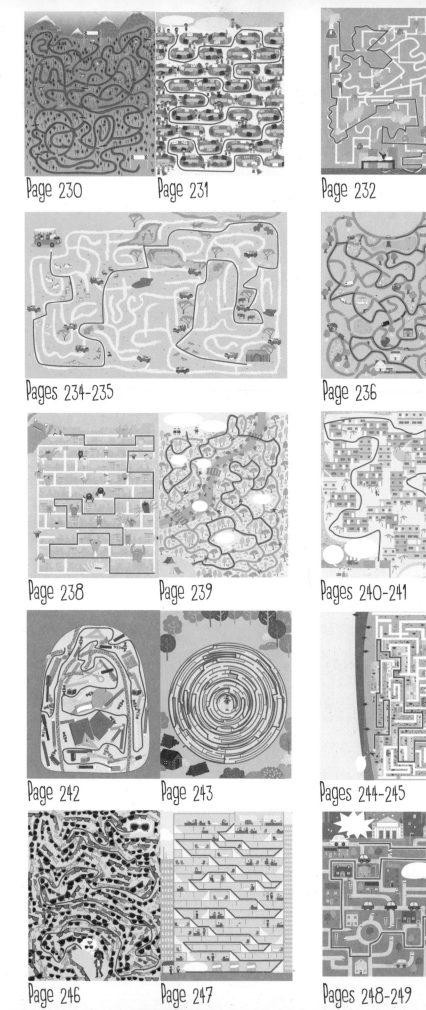

Page 230   Page 231

Page 232   Page 233

Pages 234-235

Page 236   Page 237

Page 238   Page 239

Pages 240-241

Page 242   Page 243

Pages 244-245

Page 246   Page 247

Pages 248-249